THE ILLUMINATED SOUL

RIVERHEAD BOOKS

A MEMBER OF PENGUIN PUTNAM INC.

NEW YORK 2002

THE
ILLUMINATED
SOUL

∞

ARYEH LEV STOLLMAN

RIVERHEAD BOOKS
a member of
Penguin Putnam Inc.
375 Hudson Street
New York, NY 10014

Library of Congress Cataloging-in-Publication Data

Stollman, Aryeh Lev.
The illuminated soul / Aryeh Lev Stollman.
p. cm.
ISBN 1-57322-201-1
1. Jews—Fiction. 2. Refugees—Fiction. 3. Illumination
of books and manuscripts—Fiction. I. Title.
PS3569.T6228 I44   2002   2001034916
813'.54—dc21

Printed in the United States of America

1   3   5   7   9   10   8   6   4   2

This book is printed on acid-free paper. ∞

Book design by Marysarah Quinn

Would that there were in this world no final partings.

FROM ARIHARA NO NARIHIRA, *The Tales of Ise*

stones become grapes
and figs grow from sand
Pass between lilies, thou [child] of Israel,
into the Promised Land of desire

FROM HANS HARTVIG SEEDORF,
Ahasuerus and the Plough

THE ILLUMINATED SOUL

PROLOGUE

ATELY, AN OLD FRIEND HAS reappeared, someone I loved long ago. She arrives as she did more than fifty years before, out of nowhere and out of everywhere.

I saw her in Manhattan when I spoke at the Academy of Medicine. Next she appeared at a presentation I made in Montreal. She has since come to Amsterdam and Rome, to Jerusalem and Berlin.

She arrives after everyone is seated, after I come to the podium and begin my talk. She glides easily through the dense crowds and takes a place in the back rows. Though she sits at a distance I see her distinctly. Recently, in Kyoto, where long ago

I spent a research year, the auditorium was particularly jammed. She remained standing, smiling, near an exit.

She is still the astonishing figure she was more than fifty years ago, and moves with the same youthful elegance. Her hair is still red and luxurious, at times done up in a French twist, at others in a chignon. Indoors, in the dimmest halls and auditoriums, there is a shimmer to her silken clothes, clothes that no one wore back then in my hometown, clothes one saw only in magazines or movies, worn by women waving from ocean liners or posing in exotic resorts.

When I see her I stumble for a moment in my words. She is about to ask me a question that I will not be able to answer or endure.

"Water?" someone on the dais asks me. "Are you all right, Doctor?"

I turn aside and whisper, "Yes, yes, I am all right."

I fuss with my notes. When I look up, she is gone. I do not care that she is a phantom. A conjuring trick from an aging brain. I am grateful to see her again. I am glad to imagine that after all this time she has come back to me.

CHAPTER 1

I AM AN EXPERT ON BRAINS.

For forty years I have studied the convolutions and neuronal layers where reason and consciousness reside, and the myelinated pathways that wander throughout us to encounter and perceive our world.

In my career, I have delineated several uncharted tracts within the limbic system of man, a large and complexly arching structure on the inner surface of the cerebral hemisphere. I have followed these arborlike projections from fetus to adulthood, unraveling their complex progress from point to point in the temporal lobe and beyond. I have done extensive and highly regarded work in comparative anatomy as well. I have sought and always found the equivalent structures in other mammals and even birds. All God's creatures shed light on one another. We are all variations on a theme. That so many diverse beings have so much in common should not be surprising, for, in the end, all of nature's creatures form a continuum of awareness, and a hierarchy of spirit. I am convinced of this. How else could the psalmist entreat, *Praise the Lord from the earth, wild beasts and cattle, creeping things and winged birds, kings and earthly rulers?*

M Y M O S T O R I G I N A L R E S E A R C H was performed years ago, when I worked in the laboratory endlessly, as if all of my vanishing moments, my precious here and now, might somehow be preserved in accumulating knowledge and relentless examination.

It was a most wonderful and satisfying time for me. It erased a gloom that had long been clinging to me, which I thought I would never escape.

Despite all my hard work and acknowledged success in this field of neuroanatomy I still cannot say precisely what these tracts that I have discovered actually do. I like to believe they are part of that miraculous loom on which we constantly weave back and forth and back again, where memory and time are densely laid down in the most intricate and compact way. There is no longer a "before" or "after" in these woven patterns, only a great simultaneity of recorded experience, and an audacious, if illusory, defiance of time.

But this is only conjecture.

What I do know is that my work brought me an early tenure at a respected Canadian university, and a self-satisfying amount of recognition—no more nor less than that earned by thousands of scientists in their varying endeavors.

Though I have been unable to repeat the triumphs of my earlier years, not for a lack of trying, no one has seemed to notice or care. My later work, the work of several decades, has merely been a recapitulation and refinement of my earlier discoveries. Over and over I have demonstrated similar findings in yet another specimen or another species. This is a not uncommon fate in scientific careers, and it is often concealed in lengthy curricula vitae and the endless rounds of visiting professorships and lectures at international congresses.

All my life's work has been a pale accomplishment in comparison to the great pioneers. Long ago Ramón y Cajal helped us see the mysterious unity of the myriad vertebrates, the bone-endowed sea, sky, and land creatures, called forth on the fifth and sixth days of Creation. Still others, including Purkinje, His, and Golgi, have made luminous the infinite constellations of the nervous system, discovering their components, seeking an order to their patterns, like those looking heavenward who have sought to name the stars and galaxies beyond the Milky Way.

Some say these pioneers were blessed by fortune, that

they began when the frontiers were new and so much was there to be discovered if one only looked. I find no consolation in this reasoning, nor justification for my own shortcomings and all I have not been able to achieve. I do not even believe this reasoning is true. New frontiers stand continually before us if we are wise enough to see them. We pass through one and suddenly another approaches. What we spend our lives learning will always be nothing in comparison with what remains to be discovered. The heavenly hosts, arrayed as they are in higher realms, whose eyes see so much farther than ours, sing in perpetual astonishment, *How endless are Thy works!*

I had long neglected, by the very nature of my anatomic work, the theoretical cognitive and phenomenological aspects of the mind. These are, if not truly separate, more elusive and imaginative sciences with their own special modes of observation and measurement.

Neither in my laboratory nor in my dreams have I come close to understanding the true inner workings, the spirit that hovers on the face of all living forms. What is it? I wonder. I do not know.

Yet, after a long academic life, I am suddenly in demand on account of a small book, which I wrote about the very things I do not know. I completed it in a few brief months after my retirement, when I was recuperating from surgery, too upsetting to describe here, which many times left me lying on my stomach.

The Illuminated Soul has been kindly praised by those who do the praising as "an enchanting provocation" and "a ruminative and seductive fairy tale, in which the soul is personified by a beautiful and cultivated woman, a traveler of great charm and erudition." Others have called it "cultish" and "god-denying"—though I do not believe this is true—or even "unreliable and intellectually misleading." The latter, negative attitudes have fortunately been the minority opinion and of little consequence. *The Illuminated Soul* has enjoyed a phenomenal and completely unanticipated international success.

I know it is both hubris and foolishness, but with this very success I feel a certain amount of satisfaction, pride even, a reassurance that during my time on this earth I will have left behind some trace of my existence or better still something of my imagination. Our lives and memories are otherwise such ephemeral things.

There have been other rewards as well. I have made more money in the last year than I ever made at the university. Although money never seemed to matter much to me before, I confess that in my old age I find it delightful, like the long-denied indulgence of a secret vice.

In the last year I have begun to travel extensively again, not as I once did to visit at various universities and institutes, where I would lecture about my limbic pathways with their synapses, relays, and feedback loops or tediously outline my investigative techniques. Indeed, I have put away my specimens and anatomical slides.

I travel now to talk about my little book. People ask if I find this endless touring exhausting. No. I find it exhilarating.

The crowds that come to hear me fascinate and flatter me. Each gathering of individuals, in universities, bookstores, or town halls, itself becomes one great living mind, with a sea of chattering thoughts and desires, with no definable center yet with an unmistakable community will. The crowd becomes one great "I" composed of numerous smaller "I's." Among these people I feel a rare sense of belonging, strangely delicious and comforting. I see them, feel strongly connected somehow, though I am greatly outnumbered. At the same time I have a peculiar sense of dissociation. Who am I to these people? How am I related to those others they have come to hear about, the characters in my little book? Soul and the friends I have provided for her are separate, apart from me. I barely know them anymore.

I make my usual presentation. I read of Soul's singular habits and great learning, of the worldly travels of her youth, and, in her old age, of the emissaries who constantly arrive to seek out her wisdom and knowledge, and who desire to understand who she is.

I then explain the theory I have, an intuition really, for I cannot prove it or ever hope to do so. For I believe that beneath all of our individual and cumulative thoughts, beneath our various human endeavors and cultures, our revered literatures and apprehended sciences, lies a unifying pattern, a structure too vast and too subtle to be seen. This pattern mirrors, and is mirrored within, the anatomy of our brains from which all experience must arise, and through which all things are perceived and preserved.

When my presentation is done, the questions begin.

The audience, even the most sophisticated one, does not ask much about my theory. They ask mostly about *her*, about Soul. She is mysterious, at times comforting, and in the end unobtainable. Soul has all the qualities that make one fall in love, that inspire faith and bring about our greatest joys and griefs.

The audience asks questions about the vignettes, dialogues, and the numerous illustrations I have devised, as if everything is an intentional symbol on my part rather than the unconsciously ripened fruit of imagination and memory. They turn each word and phrase over and over as in the Midrashim, the ancient and elaborate biblical commentaries that I first became drawn to in my youth and that have subtly come to influence my thinking even in my purely scientific endeavors. The audience makes connections that have never occurred to me and that I am uncertain exist though I suppose it is these very notions that prove my theory of an underlying pattern and structure.

When Soul sails down the river with her friends, why do they navigate by the movement of the vanishing clouds? Why not by the stars or the contour of the shore?

Can Soul's endless nostalgia ever be soothed by her friends? What is her yearning for?

Her menagerie is delightful, but why is the magic giraffe her favorite creature? Why not Solomon's bees, or the lovesick unicorn, or the walking fish? How did she learn their languages?

Is it really possible that she commands the aurora to appear at such a tropical latitude?

That my imaginary world is so real for others sometimes

makes me giddy, disoriented. The allotted time is quickly gone. I linger to hear yet another question. This gives the sense that I am bestowing something upon the hungry audience, though it is they who bestow on me a momentary and much needed favor. The old longing, which had flared up at my old friend's appearance, subsides.

When I am done, my brother, Asa, who always travels with me, asks, "Are you tired, Joseph? I heard it in your voice." His face is drawn and worried. After all these years of a precarious and drawn-out grace, he is blind.

I know what Asa is thinking. What will happen to him when I am gone? How will he bear being alone?

Asa has remained childlike, fearful, even in old age.

He has also learned patience.

He holds my briefcase in one hand and his white cane in the other. He does not repeat his question though it always takes me a moment to speak. He waits for my answer.

I take my briefcase from him and hold his arm.

"No, Asa, I'm fine. Don't worry."

CHAPTER 2

NE JUNE, A FEW YEARS AFTER the Second World War, a stranger appeared in our quiet border city of Windsor, Ontario. She arrived during the week of the Torah portion *Beha'alosekhoh*, which derived its name from the opening lines read that Sabbath in synagogue—*When thou lightest the lamps.*

She entered Canada on a whim, intending to visit only a few hours, then found herself stranded there, due to what she later claimed was a foolish misunderstanding of her legal status. Although this misunderstanding was of no small consequence to her or to us, in all the time she lived with us she never explained satisfactorily her apparent negligence in this regard nor did it occur to us in our own naïveté to ask. After all, she was educated and worldly, with an extraordinary record of wanderings across the globe, and with all the experience and sophistication one necessarily gathered from such voyages.

From the moment we met her we were enchanted. We could barely believe our good fortune, and good fortune, unlike bad, is rarely questioned. It was as if a heavenly being had taken on a human form as had those angels sent to Abraham's tent thousands of years before, more radiant in their physical disguise than mortals ever are, their wings barely concealed by their robes, and full of blessings and wondrous tidings. Such creatures cannot completely control their appearances either; in this respect their powers are limited. They are sent on their appointed rounds, to do what they are needed to do, and to teach us what we so desperately need to learn. Nor is everyone worthy of receiving such visitors or even seeing them. They are God's glory and majesty made visible.

Later, when the stranger was about to leave—and she left as suddenly as she arrived—we stood around the sundial in our backyard garden. She was careful to mention, looking gently from my mother to my brother, Asa, and then to me, that the misunderstanding that carried her into our lives was not one she would ever regret. Despite everything, it had brought her much joy, it had opened her eyes, and she would never forget our kindness.

She did not say these things merely to console us, or to

give us strength. Certainly she saw how heartbroken we were that she was leaving us. We were each in our way in love with her, and every heart breaks in accordance with its own private laws. Often what we believe is merely what we wish, but even after all this time I am convinced she was drawn to each of us in return and what she said was sincere. Despite her cosmopolitan and restless history and our small-town ways I believe she was happy in the summer weeks she spent among us.

I was in great pain at our parting. Some hearts know they will heal, but others, mine among them, fear they never can. Still, I did not cry. I did not dare. I was strangely ashamed of myself. Even at my father's death three years before, and I loved my father deeply, I had not felt much pain. I did not cry. I had moved through those terrible days as if I could be a living thing and never have to feel. That is why I did not judge it right or proper to cry now that the stranger was leaving us. I feared that any tears would return as witnesses against me. They would be numbered, quantified, stored up in some unknowable realm as all our deeds are, in God's in-finite memory, which, the Midrash tells us, is woven into the very substance of the stars. One day such unfilial tears would return and stand before me in glistening reproach, an open measure of my disproportionate and intemperate love.

My mother and Asa wept. My mother heaved and blew her nose into her white linen handkerchief.

Finally Asa managed to speak:

"Oh, Eva, Eva . . . why are you leaving?"

She paused a moment, then said, "I'll miss you most, Asa." Until that moment she, too, had not cried, but her eyes were now moist.

"Then why can't you stay?"

She lifted off the great square of sheer blue silk she had given him to wear over his head and eyes. It fluttered between them like a ghost. She brought her face close to his. "Now look at me carefully, Asa, so you don't forget."

Asa looked at her a long time so he would always remember her.

She smoothed his hair back. His face was damp with tears.

"You won't forget me, Asa?"

He shook his head. "No."

"Never?"

"Never, Eva."

A new wave of despair moved through me. It occurred to me that Asa's crying would only damage his weak eyes further.

Eva kissed Asa on the forehead, keeping her lips there a long time.

She is blessing him, I thought. Yes, that is why she came to us. It is her final gift. Had she not already proven her special powers, the powers of heavenly and earthly words? Perhaps Asa will see again perfectly! He will walk in the evenings and see the fireflies.

Of course this was not true. Still, looking back, I like to think she did help him somehow. After all, it took many decades before he completely lost his vision, and in that time, despite many step-wise deteriorations, he was able to do wonderful things with what remained.

Finally she embraced Asa, then my mother, and then me, one after the other, slowly, gently, and then she was gone.

CHAPTER 3

OT LONG BEFORE THE STRANGER
came to live with us, I had agreed to a great
undertaking for a boy, to prepare the weekly
Torah portions to be read aloud that summer in synagogue. I was fourteen. Rabbi
Kremlach offered to pay me ten dollars a
week, a great sum of money at the time.
Being kindhearted, the rabbi offered me
more than he would have normally on account of our family's unfortunate situation
and financial difficulties.

Mr. Zubrovsky, the regular *ba'al koreh*,
was getting married for the first time at
the age of forty. He planned to take his
new bride, Iris May, on a honeymoon to
the Holy Land. Everyone in the commu-

nity talked about their exciting itinerary and how well Mr. Zubrovsky must have been doing to afford such a trip. Mr. Zubrovsky made his real living as an accountant and worked for several people in the wealthy section of Walkerville. After the Zubrovskys' wedding, which would be held in our synagogue, they were going to catch the evening train to New York City. There the newlyweds would spend several days at the famous Waldorf-Astoria Hotel. After seeing the sights of the great city, they would board an ocean liner and travel in a luxury cabin all the way to Haifa with stops in Marseilles, France, and Piraeus, Greece.

I looked up all these places in my *Atlas of the World*. Asa, who was ten, sat next to me. He peered closely at the pages. He then turned to me.

"Joseph, do you think Mom will ever take us on an ocean liner?"

I did not think so. My father, who had been a lawyer, had been sick for several years before he died. We had no money for such luxuries as ocean liners, but I caught the pleading look on my brother's face.

"Yes, Asa. I'm sure she will."

"We never ever go anywhere interesting, Joseph. Do you really think she'll ever take us on an ocean liner? Tell me the truth."

"I don't know. Someday. It's expensive."

"When will she take us? Before it's too late? Will she take us on an ocean liner soon?"

"I don't know, Asa. Maybe soon."

IN THE GRACIOUS HYPERBOLE of those times, everyone referred to Iris May as "a lovely Toronto girl," though she was a year or two older than Mr. Zubrovsky and it was whispered that she had been married briefly and unhappily many years before. Iris May reminded me of my father in the months before he died when he grew frighteningly thin, his skin turned pale and yellow, and he began to smell like almonds. Iris May was not ill, and she did not smell of almonds, but as my mother explained she was a finicky eater and a touch absentminded, because of her "artistic temperament."

Iris May taught piano at the Royal Conservatory of Music in Toronto, and was, as my mother sadly emphasized, "a *complete* orphan, without any parents or even brothers or sisters." This distinguished Iris May's misfortune from Asa's and mine and was a subtle reminder to us boys to count our many blessings. Asa and I at least still had a mother and each other. We were not alone in the world.

Because Iris May had no immediate family the wedding was held in Windsor rather than Toronto. Mr. Zubrovsky's parents hired my mother to be the cateress. For several years my mother had been making breads and cakes for the observant members of the community. Recently Isabel Kremlach suggested that she try her hand at catering. "You have a talent for cooking, Adele. Why not use it?"

Before she knew it, my mother had been hired for two big affairs, the Zubrovsky wedding in mid-June, to be followed several weeks later by the Mizrachi Women's Summer Luncheon.

"I'm going to be working harder than before, boys," she told us. "I hope I can do everything."

Almost fifty guests attended the Zubrovsky wedding. Not only were certain members of the synagogue invited, but also several Gentile clients of Mr. Zubrovsky's. My mother wanted to make a good impression both for the sake of her new business and for the goodwill of the community. She worked in the synagogue kitchen organizing and then preparing the wedding feast, which was held in the social hall. She made pea soup, stuffed cabbage, rosemary chicken, and her fancy potatoes with garlic. There was a salad for "after the main course," which was, my mother believed, the "French way" salad was to be served. For dessert she made a fruit compote and ladyfingers.

My mother worried about all the details that could go wrong. The main entrée had to be prepared on the morning of the wedding itself so the food would not go bad. The chicken might be under- or overcooked. The roasted potatoes if not timed precisely would lose their crispness and get soggy. As for the compote, without the right amount of lemon it might turn gray. Too much lemon and it would be overly tart.

Adding to my mother's work, several days before the wedding, Iris May came from Toronto and stayed in our house. Although the Bali Hai was not far from the synagogue, Iris May was afraid to stay alone in a motel, and she could not stay with Mr. Zubrovsky's parents. Charles

Zubrovsky lived in the second-floor apartment of his parents' house, and the bride and groom were not to see each other the week before the wedding.

My mother asked me to help clean the large upstairs sunroom we usually rented to boarders but which was left unoccupied for months after our last boarder, old Mr. Applewine, had suddenly died. Though no one had slept there in all that time, my mother continued to put on fresh sheets and pillowcases every week, "in case someone comes out of the blue."

Two nights before the wedding, my mother spent hours adjusting Iris May's wedding dress. This was not one of those elaborate white gowns that younger brides wore but a long-sleeved linen suit in brownish-purple that Iris May had bought in Toronto and which she kept referring to as "the right shade of puce for my complexion." Iris May was so scatterbrained she forgot to have her outfit altered properly before she came to Windsor. She only realized her error days before the wedding when my mother was already overwhelmed with the catering. Still my mother volunteered to help fit her dress.

"But you have to do all the cooking, Adele."

"That's true, Iris May, but I'll manage. I've hired two nice young ladies to help me."

"Well, it does feel a little bunchy there, Adele." Iris May frowned in the old pier glass as my mother moved heavily around her, adjusting pins.

"I'll fix that, don't you worry, Iris May."

"I'm sorry to be such a bother but I'm afraid I'll look fat."

My mother stopped and stood with her hands on her hips. She loomed over Iris May in the mirror.

"Iris May, soon to be Mrs. Charles Zubrovsky, you will never be fat. You are thin as a stick. I'm the one who can't stop gaining, especially with all the cooking and baking I'm doing. Believe it or not, long ago I used to be slender, but never as skinny as you. You are going to look lovely."

"Well, I hope so. I'm so nervous."

"That's normal, Iris May. I was nervous, too. You're starting a new life. But I was so happy with my late husband. I miss him every day."

Iris May lowered her voice. "Yes, Adele. *You* were lucky. I saw the picture of your husband. He was very tall and handsome. But I once had a very bad experience. Very bad."

My mother thought for a moment. Finally she said gently, "Well, lightning doesn't strike twice, Iris May. I'm sure Mr. Zubrovsky will know how to make you happy. Tall isn't everything."

"Yes, but what if I get seasick on our honeymoon? I've never been on a ship. They say—"

"It's all mind over matter, Iris May. You just have to control yourself."

Iris May lowered her voice. "What if I can't have a baby?"

My mother touched Iris May softly on the shoulder. "I married late, too, Iris May. And Asa wasn't born until I was almost forty-five."

"That's what I'm saying, Adele. You were lucky."

THAT YEAR, the Sabbath *Beha'alosekhoh* coincided with the beginning of school vacation. My mother was delighted that I was asked by Rabbi Kremlach to fill in for Mr. Zubrovsky for the summer and that I had eagerly agreed to do so. Still my mother's pleasure was tempered by her concern that I might be taking on too much and by what she called my "too perfect perfectionism." Although she admitted that it was obvious I had inherited this characteristic from her, it was, in my case, "completely out of control."

She said to me, "This will be a wonderful opportunity to learn, Joseph. But I don't want you to get carried away. You always do these days. Like with the cutlery. I don't understand it."

She was referring to my latest habit of checking the kitchen drawers several times at night and making sure the knives, spoons, and forks from both our meat and dairy sets were placed in neat and exact piles. Even when I saw that this was properly done, I was afraid that something might shift as I slowly closed the drawers. The only way to be certain was to open each drawer again and check. Sometimes I found myself hovering over the drawers for half an hour or more, opening and closing them, to be absolutely sure everything stayed in order. I could not go to bed and fall asleep until I had done so.

I said, "I'm just trying to help around the house."

My mother took in a deep breath.

"Well, I don't know, Joseph. But you don't have to read the Torah *parsha* every week. Rabbi Kremlach can read some weeks, too. The Kremlachs were very kind to your father, I'll never forget that, and they have their own share of troubles, but with all due respect, Rabbi Kremlach doesn't have that much to do, really. No matter what Isabel says."

"No," I said. "I want to read every week. I can make more money that way. We need the money." That was only an excuse; I did not worry about money in those days though I knew it was a constant concern of my mother's. She worked very hard to supplement the small income she received from my father's pension.

Somehow Mr. Zubrovsky's trip and the summer Sabbaths with their series of consecutive Torah readings had formed a sort of whole in my mind. It became inconceivable to me to break up the sequence of readings, as if many things depended on me myself doing them completely. If I failed, a great danger might be involved, though I did not know what that danger was or who exactly might suffer the consequences.

ALTHOUGH AT THAT TIME the *ba'al koreh*'s duties were considered a male province, it was my mother who coached me in both the precise pronunciation and cantillation of the original biblical text. She sat with me at the dining room or kitchen table while I made my first *laynen*—reading of the weekly portion. To read a Torah scroll properly, even the most learned scholar has to review the text beforehand.

I had a leather-bound *tiykun*, a specially printed Bible almost one hundred years old that had belonged to my maternal grandfather. On each page, one column had all the vowels, punctuation, and cantillation marks clustered around the text according to the Masoretic rules passed down from generation to generation. On the facing column was the text as it appeared in a genuine Torah scroll in which the scribe wrote only the consonants with their elegantly prescribed adornments of crowns and curlicues.

My main difficulty was remembering the cantillation marks that accompanied each word, and the series of musical notes these marks represented. If I made even a minor mistake, my mother would correct me.

"*Es'naḥ'toh!*" my mother would call out, simultaneously singing and tapping out on the table the three notes embodied by this cantillation term or whichever term I had incorrectly used.

"Very good, Joseph," she would say. "Let's try it again. Okay, good. Now, once again. Good. You are almost there. The words of the Torah will become part of you. Now it's time for you to work on your own. Once you remember the music, Joseph, it's easier to remember the correct pronunciation. That's why the cantillation marks have been passed down for thousands of years, so that all the words of the Torah would be correctly pronounced. Your grandfather always said, 'Music is the handmaid of memory.'"

I would then practice diligently by myself, softly singing the passages over and over at the dining room table or sitting on the living room sofa.

When I felt I was ready, my mother would test me as I read from the unmarked column of text.

"You know it perfectly now, Joseph," she would say. "But if you make a mistake in shul Rabbi Kremlach or I can always correct you. It's nothing to be ashamed of. The only shameful thing in the world is not admitting and correcting one's mistakes." But I did not want my mother, let alone Rabbi Kremlach, correcting me in public.

That she knew the Bible so well was a great source of pride for my mother, who was otherwise a modest and self-effacing woman. My grandfather had been a *ba'al koreh*, and she was his only daughter. My grandfather, whom I only vaguely remembered, had come to Canada from Germany as a boy and had very little secular or even formal religious education. He started a small fruit business in Windsor, which was sold after he died. My mother told us how our grandfather had worked long and hard hours, but always found time to study the Bible when he came home so he could perform the duties of the *ba'al koreh* in the small congregation that had been established in Windsor. My mother had learned from sitting next to him and listening. "It was the only time I got to spend with him!" she would laugh. Then she would say seriously, "But it was a very sweet time and I still remember his saintliness. Your grandfather never raised his voice in his entire life except to read the Torah in synagogue."

Sometimes in synagogue my mother would correct Mr. Zubrovsky on the not infrequent occasions when he misread a word and no one else, not even Rabbi Kremlach, caught his mistake. Without looking up from her *chumash*, my mother would call out the correct pronunciation from the women's section, her voice suddenly and uncharacteristically high-pitched. A brief murmur of amusement would hover in the sanctuary. Mr. Zubrovsky would look toward the women's section, nod to my mother in acknowledgment, and repeat the word correctly with great ceremony and articulation.

In the social hall after services, my mother would go over to Mr. Zubrovsky, nervous that she had embarrassed him even though he was what people called a "joker," and had never shown any sign of taking offense. Still she was concerned.

"Just because people make silly jokes all the time doesn't mean they aren't sensitive inside. Sometimes it means they are extra sensitive."

Mr. Zubrovsky was very short with a thin mustache like a line just above his upper lip. With her height and weight my mother towered over him, and she unconsciously stooped a little when she spoke to him, as if to make up for this additional affront to Mr. Zubrovsky.

"Perhaps you were just tired today, Mr. Zubrovsky," she would say gently. "Everyone makes mistakes. Are you getting enough sleep? Having two important jobs like yours is so much work."

"Oh, no, I make mistakes with my eyes wide open!" Mr. Zubrovsky would blink his eyes and laugh. "But luckily I never make mistakes with money!"

Then my mother would say, as if Mr. Zubrovsky hadn't heard it all before, "Well, I hope you will forgive me, Mr.

Zubrovsky, I couldn't help myself, I am only a simple woman—"

"Not so simple!"

"Yes, thank you, but as I was saying, I really am just a simple woman but my father was a fine *ba'al koreh*. He studied hard, but he was a natural, too. It's in my blood. You would have liked each other."

"I know, I know, you don't have to explain all the time, Esther Dvorah," he'd say, flattering her by using her Hebrew names instead of Adele, as she was generally known. "Your father had you properly named. After a queen and a prophetess. And you are a wonderful cook, too! Are there any women in the Bible who were good cooks? I can't think of any!"

Then Isabel Kremlach would come over.

"Now, Adele, why are *you* blushing? There's no need to be embarrassed that you are so learned. Mr. Zubrovsky should be blushing for making such silly mistakes!"

She turned to Mr. Zubrovsky. "Am I wrong, Zubrovsky? Why aren't you blushing?"

Mr. Zubrovsky would pinch both of his cheeks with his hands.

"See, now I *am* blushing, Isabel!"

"I see. I see. That's better. Well then, how is your dear Iris May? Is she nervous about leaving Toronto? Such an artistic type will no doubt miss the big city! But I'm sure she'll have plenty of students here. We'll put a notice in the community bulletin. We are so excited to have a new face in town! It can be so dull here, you know." She touched one of the brilliant feathers on her hat. "In Havana where I grew up there were so many colorful people, so much life and music. Well, I married my sweet Kremlach and here I am." She wrung her hands in mock despair. "*¡Todo por el amor!*"

She turned to my mother. "Adele, I spoke to my Jenufa. She and her sister Olga would be happy to assist you in the kitchen and do the waitressing for our Mr. Zubrovsky's big day! They are such good girls. Have you figured out the menu?"

Before my mother could answer her, Mrs. Kremlach turned to me.

"Oh, Joseph, there you are. Can I speak with you a moment?"

She took me aside and spoke very sweetly. "What time are you coming over to visit Nebuchadnezzar? You really are a lifesaver. He's been so lonely since Ruchi went away to school."

By "school," Isabel was referring to the mental institution they suddenly sent their son, Ruchi, to that spring. I had considered Ruchi my best friend. Isabel talked as if nothing unusual had precipitated her son's departure and it had not caused her and her husband great pain. She acted as if Ruchi would be back to his usual self and home in no time.

I believed her.

Isabel continued. "Did I tell you Nebuchadnezzar said a new word this week? And at his age! He said, 'Sofa.' I guess I've been talking so much about the new one lately."

Nebuchadnezzar was the Kremlachs' Amazon parrot.

Now that Ruchi had been sent away, I was asked to visit and play with him every Sabbath afternoon. Isabel Kremlach even paid me after the Sabbath just as she would have a babysitter.

I loved how this feathery being clearly knew me, and would speak to me even if my mother insisted he did not know the true meaning of his words. I knew he was telling me something nevertheless.

Isabel Kremlach always said, "He is telling you something, Joseph. He has a brain, too. Didn't you know that?"

I suppose that is when I first began to think like a neuroanatomist. When I was with Nebuchadnezzar, I tried to imagine the size of his brain. Was it the size of a pea or the size of an almond? I would then try to look out at the world as through Nebuchadnezzar's eyes. I would squint as if this somehow was the way Nebuchadnezzar saw the Kremlachs' dining room with its elaborate table and chairs and heavy maroon draperies. I wondered, Did the green wallpaper with its raised leafy pattern remind him of the jungle where he was born? I would then cock my head and carefully look at the display cabinet that Isabel called the *vitrina*, with its painted figurines of children and animals playing within. From across the room I tried to make out the smallest details, the tiny gold buttons on the children's clothes, or the little paws and ears of the kitten playing with a ball of yarn. I had read somewhere that birds had the sharpest vision of all creatures and that certain eagles could see their prey, even little mice or skinny snakes, from a mile up in the sky. Years later when I began my anatomy career, I began by studying the optic pathways of birds, though I would do this work on the Peregrines, the order that includes the sparrows, not parrots or eagles.

At that time Nebuchadnezzar was seventeen years old, just one year older than the Kremlachs' only son Ruchi. Isabel Kremlach wore a golden bracelet with two charms on it, both engraved in Hebrew letters, one with Ruchi's real name, Yeruchem, and the other with the name Nebuchadnezzar.

Isabel Kremlach often repeated the story of her difficult pregnancies. After one of her numerous miscarriages she was so distraught her husband bought her a parrot to cheer her up.

"He always said I grew up in the jungle so it would make me happy to have such a creature. Well, I did *not* grow up in a jungle. I grew up in Miramar, the best neighborhood in Havana! As for my husband, *he* grew up in Brooklyn! But my husband's trick worked!" She would pat her belly. "Next thing you know, Ruchi was on the way. But I also consider Nebuchadnezzar to be my child."

ON THE WAY HOME from synagogue, on those occasions when she had to correct Mr. Zubrovsky, my mother would be lost in thought. She would sigh and repeat to herself the silly remark Mr. Zubrovsky had made. "'Oh, no, I make mistakes with my eyes wide open! But luckily I never make mistakes with money!'"

She would turn to us. "Some people should know better.

The words of the Torah are not to be taken lightly. They are Hashem's truth, His blueprints for the world, and we must preserve them. It is our duty. That's why we have to be careful not to mispronounce them, because then they become distorted and false." She would pause a moment to catch her breath. "Once you start tampering with the truth, all is lost. Wars have, God help us, been fought over the interpretations of single words. We all make mistakes, boys, it's human nature, but then we are obligated to correct them. That's what God expects from us."

Suddenly her eyes would fill with tears. "Sometimes I miss your father so terribly . . . He was someone I could always talk to; he understood these things."

CHAPTER 4

HE STRANGER HAD STOPPED IN Detroit during her travels across the United States. While staying downtown at the Statler Hotel, she decided to cross the border for a few hours to see another country so close by.

She woke up at dawn and took a taxi across the Ambassador Bridge.

It was an exhilarating ride high above the Detroit River. To her left, in the clear morning air, she saw the green expanse of Belle Isle floating in the band of silvery-gray water. Before her, the river curved around Essex County, flowing from Lake St. Clair to Lake Erie. This brought back sweet and unanticipated memories of a very different and distant river, the Vltava, which winds a similar course around the Josefov and Staré Město quarters of Prague, her native city.

The taxi stopped momentarily at the customs booth. The officer, who had been chatting with a colleague, peeked through the passenger window, smiled, and casually waved the car through. At the Windsor end of the bridge, the stranger paid the driver and got out of the taxi.

She then stepped onto Canadian soil.

She leisurely walked two miles along Riverside Drive until she reached Dieppe Gardens. She took pleasure in the profusion of flowers, and in particular the roses in the waterfront parks and in the yards of the houses along the way. The city council had always encouraged the citizenry to follow the example of its public spaces so that Windsor would be worthy of the name it bestowed upon itself, The City of Roses.

My father had followed this example. Born and raised in our house, my father had tended the roses and many other flowers that his own mother had long ago planted. I remember my father in the years when he was already sick, slowly walking around the yard, escorted by my mother on the first mild days of spring. All winter he had not left the house and mostly stayed upstairs in the sunroom, quietly reading or dozing in his chair. After his death, people would say he had once been a strong and vigorous man, but I only remember him as a sick man. On these occasions when he left the house after winter, my father would examine the rosebushes, and with the help of my mother, he would retie the canes of the trellis climber that formed a bower over the porch stairs. He would slowly bend over and pick up a clump of soil with his fingers.

He quoted in a hoarse voice:

" 'And the Lord God took man and put him into the Garden of Eden.' "

And my mother, her hand discreetly supporting his elbow, always completed the verse, " 'To work it and to watch it.' "

When summer arrived and the weather was warmer, he sat in the backyard near the little sundial, which lay in a semicircle of peonies and marigolds. "Adele," he would whisper as she helped him into a chair, covering him with a light blanket, "you have brought me into Paradise!"

While my father was alive I had not given much thought to our garden, but after he died I suddenly inherited his interest and love for it, though for some reason I was only enthusiastic about the roses. The other flowers seemed to me to be out of place. I went to the public library and read everything I could find on the cultivation of roses. I began following Monsieur Charcot's weekly gardening column in the *Star*. From time to time there were newly developed hybrids that Monsieur Charcot would trumpet. Monsieur Charcot would always begin these special columns with "Shhh! Can you keep a secret? Now I shall reveal to you my latest love affair!"

I would ask my mother to buy me various new bushes I had read about to expand and improve our garden. At first my mother hesitated.

"Joseph, your father enjoyed all the different flowers we have. I hate to change the things he liked. Where will you put any more roses?"

I persisted. In the end, my mother gave in to my relentless appeals. She rubbed her forehead in a gesture of defeat.

"You'll have to take care of them yourself, Joseph. I don't know much about roses. Your father always took care of them. He learned from his mother. Well, I suppose I should be glad you are interested in them, too."

My mother would then take me to the nursery and follow me along the aisles while I carefully made my choices. She nodded approval at each of my decisions. She chatted with Mr. and Mrs. Posner, the owners, who told us about the various specimens, both bare-rooted and potted, that were not yet in bloom.

Sometimes my mother addressed the Posners as Mr. and Mrs. Peony since she said their faces were round and pink and healthy-looking.

"I mean it as a compliment, you know," she would say. "Peonies are actually my favorite flower, even more than roses."

"Yes, Mrs. Ivri, we know," Mrs. Posner would say. "And you, of course, remind us of a hollyhock because you are so tall!"

My mother would laugh. "Yes, but I'm no longer so slender! Well, anyway, Joseph is intolerant of the other flowers. Last season he dug out the marigolds to plant the previous roses we bought. Now I'm afraid the peonies are in mortal danger."

"They have lots of ants," I said.

"Now, Joseph," Mrs. Posner said, "you should not be so critical of all the other flowers. God made them all. It says so in the Bible. And the ants are industrious creatures. We can always learn from their ways. Meanwhile we'll throw in this extra bush with the two you already chose. It got mixed up with the others and we don't know what it is or even what color, so you might as well take it. It will be a surprise!"

I did not like the idea of taking a plant, even a rosebush, that would be a surprise. Monsieur Charcot had often emphasized that the proper balance of color and hardiness was essential to good taste. What if this bush was a weak or impure hybrid with an unsuitable ancestor? What if it did not match the others? But I was too embarrassed to decline the Posners' generosity.

Despite her acts of resistance, and professions of ignorance, my mother always came outdoors and watched as I did my plantings, offering valuable advice. "No, not there, Joseph. It's too shady," or "Joseph, don't plant them so deep. The roots will suffocate." Sometimes she betrayed a more sophisticated taste and memory. "I think its color would be wonderful over there, next to the one your father planted the year Asa was born. I have never seen such a wonderful pink."

CHAPTER 5

T HAT JUNE THE STRANGER AR-
rived, the roses all over the county were
especially abundant and vivid. The Naughty
Margarets were intense scarlet, the Gracious Majesties were golden yellow, and
even the locally developed hybrid *Bonjour,
grandes soeurs!* were silvery-white. The
bushes along the border of our yard and
along the walkway participated in this colorful and unprecedented grandeur. The
trellis climber over our porch stairs was so
lavishly covered with heavy red blooms
that you could barely see our front door
from the street. Throughout the city, the
fragrance of roses was everywhere and

rich, conquering the sour-mash smell that often hovered from the distillery.

Various letters were printed in the *Star* about these wonderful phenomena of color and fragrance. Some readers attributed them to the extra rain we had that spring and others to the mildness of the previous winter.

Asa carefully read these opinions. One afternoon he announced he was going to send his own letter. He asked me to type it on my father's typewriter. "Typing is nicer, Joseph. I wish I knew how to type like you. My handwriting is getting worse and worse. Mrs. Faybach said so."

Asa believed that the phenomena of the roses were due to storms on the sun.

I thought he came to his odd conclusion because of what was happening to his retinas, and the great fear that had taken hold of him. During the previous year, when he was nine, his vision had slowly and subtly begun its deterioration. At first he stumbled at night in the darkness. He kept a flashlight near his bed. "It's so black out, Joseph," he would say. Both my mother and I thought he was merely frightened of the dark or was having nightmares. Naively, we still did not realize anything was seriously wrong until he began having trouble adjusting from outdoor to indoor light. When he came indoors from the bright sunshine, he stood still for several minutes in the hallway until he could see.

My mother took him to Dr. Fairclough, our family doctor. "Do you think Asa needs glasses?" my mother asked.

"I don't know what it is," Dr. Fairclough told my mother,

looking into Asa's eyes. "But he needs more than glasses. He needs to see a specialist. I will call someone in Detroit."

My mother took us to see the eye doctor in Detroit. Dr. Fairclough had suggested that I go along so that my eyes could be checked as well.

In the doctor's examination room was a large poster illustration of a retina. Red arteries and blue veins spread out from the center of the retina like the roots of a great tree seen from below, by something sinister living deep in the earth.

The doctor examined Asa and me. The doctor found a few brownish deposits on the edges of the retinas when he looked into Asa's eyes. My eyes were normal.

The doctor then asked my mother several questions:

Did anyone else in the family have trouble with their eyes? Had any grandparents or any aunts and uncles gone blind?

The questions were like blows. When my mother heard the word "blind" she pressed her hand against her chest and had to stop and catch her breath. Still she tried diligently to answer these useless inquiries.

She could think of no one in her family or my father's who had gone blind. Later she wrote to a cousin of my father's who lived in Paris and to another one who lived in Miami. They wrote back. No one remembered such a case in the family.

It made no difference. The doctor had told my mother that Asa could go slowly blind, though he might have useful, even good, day vision for many years and perhaps decades to come. He could still see and read perfectly in good lighting and for now he could go to regular schools. No one could predict precisely the time course of the disease. With a little care and planning he would live a productive and happy life. "No use worrying too much about it now," he said.

The doctor recommended that Asa wear sunglasses outdoors in bright sunlight, to protect his retinas and preserve their nerve cells, and to help him adjust to the abrupt change from outdoor to indoor light.

"Asa needs to find the right balance of light," the eye doctor said.

As my mother believed in telling only the truth, she did not purposely hide the ominous facts about his eyesight from Asa when he asked her. Still, she always tried to be optimistic and did not believe this in any way contradicted her strict observance of the truth. "Hope is another word for faith," she confided in me, "and so I'm still telling Asa the truth."

Every day Asa asked her what the doctor had said and every day she repeated to Asa that he might have good day vision for many years to come. Still he had to be careful and wear sunglasses in bright sunlight. He needed to find the right balance of light.

"I don't want to go to school for those blind children."

My mother would try to reassure him, "You don't have to now."

"Not 'now' but when?"

"Maybe never, sweetheart."

" '*Maybe* never'?"

"Probably never."

Asa began to panic. A series of contradictory ideas took hold of him.

At first he refused to go outdoors in the sunshine even with his prescribed sunglasses. "The sun is destroying my eyes!" he cried.

On sunny days I had to walk with him to school holding his hand while he kept his eyes completely shut. He would not open them until he was indoors.

Just before the stranger came to live with us, at the approach of summer with its warmer weather and longer days, he went around the house every morning pulling down the window shades to keep out the sunlight. As this made the house too dark for him to see, he turned on all the lamps. This made the house very depressing for my mother.

"Really, Asa, the house is so gloomy," she said. "Human beings need natural light."

Finally my mother came to a compromise with Asa. On sunny days he could close the blinds in every room of the house except for the kitchen where my mother did most of her work, her bedroom, and the sunroom upstairs.

"I need some sunlight on each floor or I get sad," she said.

Asa then had a new idea, which was particularly upsetting for my mother. On some days, and these times were unpredictable, Asa would not use his eyes. He called these times his Daylight Savings Days. He would keep his eyes shut as much as possible. "This way my eyes won't get used up so quickly," he said. On his Daylight Savings Days he wore a blindfold everywhere, in case he opened his eyes accidentally. He took little steps, groping his way around the house or hovering near my mother or me. One morning he asked my mother to buy him a cane like the one old Mr. Glantz in the synagogue carried. "No, sweetheart," she would whisper to hide the tremor in her voice. "You don't need a cane, sweetheart."

"But I need to practice!"

"You don't need to practice."

"Yes, I do!"

My mother said to me, "Joseph, I'm at my wit's end. I don't know what to do with Asa. His vision is still very good. There is so much he can see and enjoy. The doctor said so. Try to encourage him to look at things. Show him things in your books. Asa's always interested in what you're doing. Are you listening to me, Joseph? It may be years before Asa is completely—"

She would then suddenly excuse herself. "I have to get back to the kitchen." She would make a great commotion with her pots and pans and bowls. When I came into the kitchen to investigate, she would look up and I knew that she had been crying.

IN HIS LETTER to the Star, which I typed for him, Asa explained that the light on earth had changed that year, "because of terrible storms in the sun's atmosphere."

The previous year there were several reports in the news about the great solar storms which were causing magnificent auroras to be seen at much lower latitudes than usual, over

Hudson Bay and Prince Edward Island. At times the immense waves of magnetic particles interfered with radio and telegram transmissions across the Pacific Ocean and the North Pole. Although the newspapers had reported that these conditions were due to a predictable eleven-year cycle of sun activity which was already waning, Asa came up with his own elaborate theory from which he could not be dissuaded.

Asa believed that these storms were caused by a bad comet that crashed into the sun. The light of the sun had become dangerous because it was mixed with the light of a bad comet. Only another comet could change things back.

"It's true, Joseph. Plants and flowers and some people's eyes like mine are very sensitive to these things. That's why I'm going blind and the roses are so pretty. Maybe one day the light will change back to the way it was if another comet crashes into the sun and pushes the bad comet out. Do you think that will happen, Joseph? Do you think a good comet might crash into the sun and push the bad comet out?" He showed me an elegant drawing he had made of the sun with a large comet whizzing by. "I don't care what happens to the stupid roses. I hate them."

He was pleading with me to agree with him. I was filled with such sorrow that my chest hurt. He knew deep down he was powerless, that there was nothing he could do to help himself. It was how I often felt about myself.

I looked at Asa a long time. I remember thinking, My little brother is so beautiful. Sometimes strangers would stop us on the street to ask his name. I could tell they were sim-

ply trying to get a better look at him. My mother rarely referred to Asa's appearance though I knew she was aware of
it, too.

I told myself, I am proud of Asa's beauty. I sought to convince myself, No, no, I am not jealous that there is no such
beauty in me.

In the previous year I had grown rapidly. I had become
tall, bone-thin, and clumsy like Iris May and even like my father before he died when he would call to me in his hoarse,
shriveling voice, "Joseph, do you want to sit near me awhile?
Asa is sitting here, too. Would you like to join us and draw
something together?"

"No," I would say, "I'm busy. I have lots of homework." I
could not bear to look at or even listen to my father anymore.

"Would you like me to help you with your homework?"

"No, that's okay. I can do it myself." I was ashamed of my
behavior, but I could not help myself.

Now, I told myself over and over again, I accept my lot.
There must be a reason for my ugliness. I developed my own
distorted theory about physical beauty.

I came to the conclusion that God did not squander
beauty. He gave out his gifts measuredly and with a purpose,
often as a compensation for something terrible. This elaborate theory of my own worked as a sort of consolation for
me. I could not believe in a world that was so unfair, a world
without a mechanism of justice for all of its creatures. As a
corollary to this theory I believed that because I was not
beautiful I would somehow be safe from some of the terri-

ble things that happened to other people. I would not go blind like my brother Asa, or wither and turn yellow like my father. I would be happy someday even if I was not happy then. I would repeat these various points over and over in my mind until I exhausted myself. Despite these efforts, I still worried and doubted my theory. I could not avoid the obvious exceptions that I encountered. Being homely did not seem to make people like Iris May happy.

"Do you think another comet might come, Joseph, and push the bad comet out? Mommy said I should ask your opinion since you know science. She said she doesn't know about these things, so she can't say."

"Yes, Asa, I think so. I think so."

"Do you think it will happen soon? Before I'm completely blind?"

"Yes, I think it might happen soon. There are lots of comets in outer space. Another one is bound to crash into the sun soon."

"Will you finish typing my letter now?"

CHAPTER 6

ROM DIEPPE GARDENS, THE
stranger walked a short distance along
Ouellette Avenue, the main thoroughfare,
peering into the better downtown shops.

At Feld's Jewelry she saw a ruby
bracelet in the window display.

Greta Feld would later tell my mother,
"First thing in the morning, your young
lady boarder came into our store and
bought the bracelet from the Kalkstein estate. Didn't you recognize it?"

My mother did not.

"You don't remember it? Old Shooshy
only wore it on Rosh Hashonah. Your
boarder found it irresistible. She even looked
at it with her own magnifying glass. Can

you imagine carrying your own magnifying glass in your handbag? And what a big handbag! What does she have in there?"

"The bracelet is just lovely on her," my mother said.

"I knew you'd say that, Mrs. Never-say-anything-bad-about-a-person. But you know what I'm really asking, Adele. I'm amazed she bought it even if I priced it too low, since she had to take rooms with you. She acted very casual, but I think she knew she got a steal. I thought I knew my gems but this time I must have made a big mistake. My husband, may he rest in peace, would never have been so foolish.

"So what is she like? Are you getting along? What does she do with her time? Does she have any plans?"

While she waited for my mother to answer, Greta Feld adjusted her wig, which always sat awkwardly on her head. Her own hair had fallen out permanently the day she received the news that her son had been killed in Normandy.

"Eva keeps very busy, Greta. She's finishing her father's book. She promised him she would. He was a great scholar, and she certainly is her father's daughter. I'm learning so much from her."

"Is that so?"

"Yes, and she's even teaching Asa Japanese calligraphy. His handwriting has been so terrible lately. I don't understand it since he draws so well. But the calligraphy is making him more confident and his handwriting is already improving. Anyway, Eva speaks six"—my mother began counting on her thick fingers—"no, I mean seven languages. I almost forgot Czech. She's very European that way, you know."

"Yes, I know, Adele. They all speak twenty languages. That's why they have so many wars!"

My mother smiled nervously. "Eva is a remarkable young woman, and stunning, too."

Mrs. Feld said, "That's the way it is with refugees nowadays. Even if they're poor as church mice they look and act for all the world like countesses. They have a few valuable things, which they miraculously turn into piles of cash!" She lowered her voice. "I know I shouldn't say this but I've heard that some of them have had to do terrible things to survive."

"Really, Greta. That is an awful thing to say. May God forgive you. These people have all lost so much in the war."

"And I haven't?"

THE STAR'S Geneviève LaFontaine also saw the stranger that first day as she walked down Ouellette Avenue. Weeks later Geneviève LaFontaine would write in her popular weekly column, "N'est-ce pas?":

> *Every day we encounter people to whom we never give a second thought. But one early morning, quite by chance, I saw a remarkable creature looking dreamily into Lazare's Furs even though it was such warm weather. She carried the most brilliant parasol. It was a sunny day. She stood there, so statuesque and regal, one foot turned out ever so slightly. Of course, I went right over to her and asked if she was new in Windsor. All she said*

*was, "I'm just visiting for a few hours. What a pretty
town you have." I never thought we would cross paths
again. I never dreamed of such a story filled with so
much romance and tragicalness!*

The stranger enjoyed her excursion to Canada and was
ready to return across the border.

The United States would not let her back.

She had violated her single-entry visa.

"Perhaps the consul can help you," the customs officer at
the United States border said gravely. He sent her back to
Windsor where somehow they allowed her to reenter.

In the years after the war, before its operations were
transferred to Toronto, there was still an American consulate
in Windsor. She took the elevator to its offices on the sixth
floor of the Guaranty Trust building at the corner of Victoria and University.

The consul, Mr. Meadowlark, a small, carefully groomed
man, listened patiently to her predicament.

From time to time Mr. Meadowlark looked curiously at
her papers and up at her again.

"I'm truly sorry, young lady. There's nothing I can do. It's
our law. You have sadly lost your welcome. Of course, you
can always reapply, but the paperwork could take quite
some time, months or years as you well know. All sorts of
people are trying to come to us and we have to be careful,
especially nowadays with the communist threat. Would you
like to reapply?"

"But that is so difficult. Is there anything else that can be done? Perhaps you could advise me."

He then smiled at her. "This is not such a bad place to find yourself in, young lady. No, not at all. As you can see, the Canadians are casual about foreigners these days. They can be quite sloppy about their borders. Otherwise I do not know what would have happened to you. My wife and I have lived here happily for several years, though we're not stuck like you. We drive our Buicks back and forth all the time. We have two!"

" 'Buicks'?"

"They're American cars. I think married couples should be independent, don't you?"

She was silent.

"Is that scent frangipani?"

"No."

He looked at her carefully. He cleared his throat. "Sometimes my wife goes away for several days to visit her family in Chicago. As a matter of fact she's in Chicago now and has left me all alone. Next week I'll be driving across the border to join her. Of course, my car is never searched at the border. I could smuggle the crown jewels across if I was the criminal type and had the right motivation." He stared at her. "But I'd need some incentive to do something like that."

She was silent again.

"I see. Of course. You were on your way across America. May I ask if you have any resources? Will you be all right? I only ask out of personal concern. Of course, it's not my business and you do not have to tell me."

"I am an independent person. I would never be a burden on your government." She held firmly to her large handbag.

"Oh, that's good. How so?" He smiled brightly. His teeth were very crooked. He waited for her to say something more. "Oh, you are a very reserved young lady, aren't you? Shyness has its charms but sometimes makes things difficult for a person."

She looked at him. She did not speak.

He gathered up various papers on his desk.

"Well, perhaps it's a little dull here, young lady, but the streets are friendly. If you find it too dreary you can always move east to the bigger cities, Toronto or Montreal. They're very lively. As I said, we have applications here if you want to fill them out. It seems there's nothing else I can do for you." His voice changed. He now spoke coldly. "Is there anything else you wish to say?"

The stranger did not argue or plead for help.

Would it in fact have been so hard for the American consul to look the other way? To let her somehow return quietly across the river in the passenger seat of his Buick, even without "the right motivation" or "incentive"? She had committed no crime. There had only been a foolish misunderstanding about her visa.

Instead, she thanked Mr. Meadowlark for his time. He walked behind her to the door.

She rode down the elevator and left the building.

What was she to do now? Where should she go? What about her trunk that was still at the Statler Hotel in Detroit?

She looked up.

High above Windsor a great circle of clouds had come to rest, which did not cast shadows that she could see, nor did it in any way detract from the brilliance of the morning. If there were a heavenly counterpart to our city perhaps this ring of clouds would have been its border.

She took the circle of clouds as a gracious sign, for it recalled the verse that she knew well:

And in the place where the cloud abode, there the Children of Israel encamped.

And so, despite her lack of connections to anyone in our town, or knowledge of its ways, the stranger decided then and there, standing on the sidewalk in the warm afternoon, to make the best of things. She would not move on to Toronto or Montreal. She would not reapply for an American visa. She was where she was. She had already traveled so much. Perhaps in this very place she might find a new home. The moment she was settled, she would send to Detroit for her trunk.

She made a few inquiries of passersby on what were indeed then friendly streets, and soon was escorted along several blocks of old houses partially hidden by the broad canopies of trees. She was delighted and heartened by the splendor of the deciduous foliage, for in every leafy bough she saw the arm of providence.

Later she would tell us, she could not for the life of her remember who it was who accompanied her those several blocks. This upset her greatly.

Was it a man or a woman?

Was the person young or old?

As far as she knew, she never saw this person again. Although people might smile at her from across the street or wave hello, and at that time people in Windsor did this whether they knew you or not, no one ever approached her to ask, "Remember me from the day you arrived? It was a magnificent day. How did you make out?" Nor could she then answer and say, for she was meticulously polite and feared the sin of ingratitude, "Yes, you were most kind to me then. I've wanted so much to thank you again. Perhaps I neglected to do so properly at the time."

But it is often the fate of those who are sent to help us to remain hidden and unrecognized. Or, better said, it is our fate, and a cause of inestimable sadness in this world, that we cannot recognize these sweet messengers or find them again. They are of the same substance as dreams. They are the fingers of God.

In this instance, before disappearing, the finger pointed to our house on the corner of Victoria and Montrose.

"Here we are, Madame. They have a room. You'll be welcome."

At that moment the roses on the porch trellis and along the footpath swayed in a lingering breeze, welcoming her in their own fragrant language.

"Oh, thank you!"

Later she would teach us that even flowers and trees have souls, as we are told in the Midrash.

"How else could wise King Solomon speak to them?" she

asked us. "He wouldn't have much conversation with them if they didn't have souls."

Another time she would say to me, "Isn't it wonderful, Joseph, to know your roses love you in return, that they're happy to see you, that they are blessing you for your kindness?"

CHAPTER 7

S HORTLY   BEFORE   THE   FIRST
World War, a lengthy article appeared in
the academic journal *Biblische Monatsschrift*. This essay was written in the scholarly German of the day and had the
unwieldy title "Ursprung und Wanderschaften der übernatürlichen Wolken durch
die Wüste und uralte Literatur"—"Origin
and Peregrinations of the Supernatural
Clouds Through the Wilderness and Ancient Literature."

The essay's young author, Enoch Laquedem, had completed his university studies
in Vienna, Berlin, and Heidelberg. Laquedem was descended from an old and

wealthy Prague family. His grandfather and father owned land and phosphorite mines in Bohemia, and so he was able to pursue his education with great dedication and thoroughness.

As a student, Enoch Laquedem had been drawn to that remarkable tradition that began to flower in the nineteenth century, the so-called *Wissenschaft des Judentums*, the Science of Judaism, which arose out of the Jewish Emancipation and Enlightenment.

Among many cultural and historical endeavors, the Science of Judaism made great strides in understanding the origins of Hebrew and its relation to other ancient Near Eastern languages. The Bible was analyzed as were postscriptural texts, most significantly the Talmud and the elaborate biblical commentaries of the Midrash.

The scholars of the *Wissenschaft des Judentums* came from various religious denominations and backgrounds, both Jewish and Christian, religious and secular. Though it was called a science, often what the scholars sought were ways to prove their own modern ideas. They sought a better understanding of their own lives and culture.

In his first published essay, which appeared in the *Biblische Monatsschrift*, Enoch Laquedem traced the origins of the two mysterious cloudlike phenomena that God had sent to guide and support His people in the wilderness: the Pillar of Cloud that appeared each day to lead the Children of Israel through the desert, and the second similar manifestation of God's providence, the Cloud of Glory that covered the Holy Tabernacle.

In an attempt to understand their symbolic significance to

the ancient mind, Enoch Laquedem sought out and compared other references to atmospheric phenomena in the ancient literature of Mesopotamia as well as in the Bible itself. He demonstrated that the ancient world was rich in language and depictions of these phenomena. He quoted from the Canaanite epic of Rahab, the Prince of the Sea who was challenged by the "Lord who rode on *arabhoth*—clouds." From Genesis he cited the verse concerning the *ayd*, the mist that rose in Eden to water the land, and also the *anan*, the cloud in which God set His rainbow after the flood. And preceding all these in antiquity and primordial power was the *ruah Elohim*, the wind from God that swept over the waters at Creation.

THE THEME OF CLOUDS and natural phenomena, which obsessed Enoch Laquedem throughout his scholarly life, governed his personal life as well.

Young Enoch Laquedem first saw his future wife, Charlotte Marie, floating on an artificial cloud, as she sang the role of Seraphina in the new opera *Vom Himmel Gefallen—Fallen from Heaven*—which premiered at the Estates Theater in Prague. Decades later when I visited that city, I came across an original copy of the libretto and score at the library of the Academy of Music.

In the first scene of this now-neglected work, the Marquis of Auerbach, returning from the hunt, falls from his horse and suffers a concussion. Upon awakening, he finds himself in possession of a new and heightened perception. Opening his eyes, the marquis looks up and in his astonishment sees the beautiful Seraphina high above the stage, hovering in a billowing vapor, accompanied by six cherubs from the St. Michael's Boys Choir. At first the marquis assumes he has died and arrived in heaven, but as he cautiously and somewhat sensuously feels his chest and limbs, he realizes that he is indeed still alive.

The marquis cries out:

> *Ich habe mich in einen Engel verliebt!*
> *I have fallen in love with an angel!*

The tall, ethereal Seraphina, standing on her hidden platform, answers with a lovely, coquettish modulation from C minor to G major:

> *Oh, but you mustn't.*
> *I will only disappoint you.*
> *We angels spend*
> *so little time on Earth.*

The marquis will not give up and, with his new sensory powers, pursues his love. In the end, Seraphina, against all natural laws of the heavens, finds herself falling in love with the handsome and persistent nobleman.

Before the close of the opera she prays to God to allow her to become mortal.

> *Für diese unsterbliche Flügel—*
> *For these immortal wings*

paired and translucent,
for their divine substance,
I do thank You,
but even so I humbly beg—
Transform me, transform me!
to that other race
in Your image so wondrously fashioned
and of eternal love forged

Like the Marquis of Auerbach, young Enoch Laquedem pursued and married his cloud-borne angel.

His elderly parents were unhappy with this match for their only son. A singing actress was a frivolous and unreliable creature, certain to break his heart and ruin his life. Nevertheless, when they saw how determined their son was, they gave their consent.

Together Enoch and Charlotte Marie had a child, Eva. But the former Seraphina was not suited to be the wife of an earth-bound scholar. One day she simply disappeared, leaving forever her four-year-old daughter and distraught husband.

Enoch Laquedem found her hastily scribbled note on the desk in his study.

My dear Enoch,
    Please try to understand and to forgive me. Do not
be afraid to be without me. You have our little Eva. I
am not afraid of the future. I will remain as always,
                    Your heavenly Lotte

For a year or two, Laquedem was unable to do his textual research properly or to write. Though his family was wealthy and he did not need to work, he decided he needed distraction. He took a position as a librarian and manuscript curator for the Prague Jewish Museum, which had been established at the beginning of the century in the Staré Město quarter, in two rooms of a house on Benediktská Street. Over time the Jewish Museum would grow to include several synagogues, the Old Jewish Cemetery, and the Jewish Town Hall. Augustin Laquedem, Enoch's father, had been a supporter of the museum from its founding.

Enoch Laquedem was well suited for his position. Not only was he educated in Hebrew, Aramaic, and other relevant languages, but he grew up with a special understanding and feeling for rare books and manuscripts. His family, to which he was sole heir, had a small but outstanding collection of rare books and illuminated manuscripts, the most precious of which was the magnificent *Augsburg Miscellany*, which had been in the Laquedem family for generations.

With time Enoch Laquedem began to recover from his abandonment by Charlotte Marie and went on to write prolifically. He published articles, treatises, and monographs on subjects from philology to historical philosophy. He turned increasingly to the ancient commentaries of the Midrash, which fascinated him with their interweaving of the disparate texts that made up the Bible.

He translated and published, at his own expense, the single extant copy of a Midrash on Esther compiled by an obscure, twelfth-century Spanish scholar and contained in the *Augsburg Miscellany*. For the Jewish Museum, he composed an updated bibliography of all the rare books and manuscripts in its collection.

Just before the Second World War, Laquedem came back to the subject of his first published article, "Origins and Peregrinations," incorporating and expanding the varied themes of both language and the power of nature into his magnum opus, *Clouds of Glory*.

In his introduction to this now lost work, Enoch Laquedem wrote:

> *That the Bible is a perfected writing is not disputed. This should not give us pause if we believe it is Divinely dictated, but if the writings of the Bible are works of man, they speak to us in their perfection of an artistic tradition that had developed over many centuries. As the embryo of each modern human develops through stages resembling more ancient creatures, the fish, amphibians, and so forth, so the language and literature of the Bible carries within it more ancient linguistic and literary forms that are mostly lost to us.*

The evening before Eva left Prague, Enoch Laquedem gave his daughter the unfinished, handwritten manuscript of *Clouds of Glory*.

"Perhaps, if I am not deluding myself, *Clouds of Glory* will be the most important achievement of my life, with the exception of you, my beloved daughter. You must finish it for me."

"But why don't you come with me, Father? There is still time. Chujo can help you, too."

"I can't. I've told you before. There are too many things I must do. I have my duties. I can't leave now."

"But what must you do?"

As always he would not say. But Eva knew he was devoted to the museum and afraid for its survival.

"But, Father, you cannot imagine there is anything you can do for the museum. It is already too late. It will be destroyed. And how will I be able to finish your book? Father, you must come with me if only to finish it yourself. Your duty is to your book and yourself."

"I will try to join you later. But if not, you know my thinking better than anyone. I have always discussed everything with you. You will know how to finish my book. Will you promise me?"

"But, Father, how—"

"Will you promise me?"

"I promise, Father."

She then said, "Let me take the *Augsburg Miscellany* with me. Otherwise they will surely take it from you. It will be destroyed."

"No. It's too dangerous. You know it is forbidden to take valuables out of the country. If you are caught, they might kill you."

"I'm not afraid, Father."

"I know you're not afraid, Eva,"—he took her hands and kissed them—"but it is terrible enough that you must leave me, too. I could not survive another moment if I lost you forever, with no hope of seeing you again. I will not allow you to risk your life for parchment and ink."

"But, Father, it is not just parchment and ink. It has inspired you so greatly. You have always said so. We must do whatever we can to save it. Everything else we have will be destroyed."

"I forbid you. We are not permitted to risk our lives for material things."

Eva could not bear to think that the miscellany might be confiscated and burned. Everyone knew that precious books and great libraries were in flames everywhere. Wasn't it her duty to save the manuscript now that she was able to leave her homeland? There was nothing she could do to rescue the rest of her father's library.

The night before she left, while her father was sleeping, Eva disobeyed her father. She took the *Augsburg Miscellany* from the cabinet in the library and hid it among the few belongings she was allowed to take with her. Miraculously, she was never caught by the authorities.

When Eva told us this, my mother said in an astonished voice, "You were so brave!"

"Not really, Adele. I wasn't brave. I just found I wasn't afraid. I was forced to leave my home. My father would not come with me. I had tried so many times to persuade him. What more did I have to lose? It was my duty."

"But what about your husband?"

"Chujo was not afraid of anything. He encouraged me. He gave me strength."

And so, from her homeland, Eva Laquedem carried these two treasures, *Clouds of Glory* and the *Augsburg Miscellany*, everywhere she traveled around the dangerous world. They never left her side, neither by day nor by night, until she brought them into our home.

CHAPTER 8

HE DOORBELL RANG.

From the living room sofa, I saw my mother moving toward the front hall, though I could not see the front door itself.

"Why didn't you answer the door, Joseph?"

"I'm practicing the *parsha*. I'm almost done."

"All right. When you're ready, we'll go over everything. I wonder who it could be? I'm not finished with my cake orders."

I still remember the verse I was reading then. I can even hear the cantillation notes accompanying the words in my mind:

"*Asei lekhoh sh'tai ḥatzotzros kesef . . .*

Make yourself two trumpets of silver, of hammered work shall you make them."

I looked up as my mother opened the door.

A small pool of sunlight filled the front hall. It was a soft and spreading light that divided into two broad bands as the person on the porch came closer to the threshold. For a moment I had the strange and powerful illusion that these two bands of light were the silvery trumpets that God commanded Moses to make for the calling of assemblies and for the journeying of the camps in the wilderness. They seemed so real they frightened me. I thought I might be going crazy. I knew that crazy people sometimes saw things that weren't there.

The silver trumpets vanished.

Asa was noisily feeling his way along the dining room table, tapping the wooden surface loudly with his hands. It was one of his Daylight Savings Days, and he was keeping his eyes closed and blindfolded.

Asa then groped along the walls and came up behind my mother.

"Mom, who is it?"

My mother stood there with a startled look on her face. For a moment I thought something was wrong. Maybe a robber was at the door. There had been two robberies in Windsor in the last weeks. The local police could not find the culprit and said the perpetrators might be people coming over from Detroit.

Again Asa asked, "Mom, who is it? Is anyone there? You didn't say hello!"

"Yes, yes, there is someone here," she said in a hushed voice, turning to Asa. She then looked back toward the doorway. "Forgive me. I'm so sorry. I just wasn't expecting . . . anyone. My cakes . . ." My mother smiled. "Well, I suppose now I'm not making any sense. May I help you?"

I heard the stranger's voice before I saw her. Her voice was familiar and strange at the same time. The *s*'es were high and sibilant and the *t*'s and *d*'s were like rapid clicks. I thought she might be from England.

"Hello. My name is Eva Higashi. I was told you might have rooms available?" She said this like a question, but softly and sweetly.

I came over from the living room.

The moment before I actually saw her face and form, there was a most wonderful color, a shimmering blue-green with glints of gold like the head and wing feathers of Nebuchadnezzar.

"Higashi?" My mother paused. "You're not from here, are you? I'm Adele Ivri. This is Asa, my baby. Joseph, my eldest, is studying in the living room. Oh, here he is." My mother wiped her hands on her apron. "I'm so sorry, I was just baking cakes in the kitchen."

"It smells delicious in here. There is no reason to apologize for that."

My mother blushed and smiled shyly. I thought she looked like one of her girlhood pictures that hung in her bedroom.

My mother then said, "Boys, you mustn't stare!" But she was staring, too.

"I'm not staring," Asa said. "How can I be staring? My eyes are closed!"

"Asa, please. Not so loud." She turned to the stranger. "Why don't you please come inside?"

"Thank you. Thank you so much. I'm so sorry to intrude."

"Oh, you are not intruding," my mother said.

Eva Higashi looked back and forth at each of us, smiling as if we were the most fascinating and delightful creatures she had ever seen. She tilted her head slightly as she came through the doorway. She was surprisingly tall, even taller than my mother, her thick red hair almost brushing against the lintel.

She gently closed the door behind her.

I had never seen anyone so glamorous and elegant. Her high heels and folded parasol matched the marvelous color of her dress. She placed one foot in front of the other, carefully, as if she were crossing a narrow bridge from a mysterious and enchanted world we knew nothing about, into our small and quiet one.

"What does she look like? Is she pretty?" Asa asked.

"Asa," my mother said, blushing. "What kind of question is that? Why don't you take off your blindfold and see for yourself?"

"I can't. It's my Daylight Savings Day." Asa asked again, louder, "What does she look like?"

I was embarrassed by Asa's behavior. I could not remember being embarrassed by Asa before, even when I had to walk him to school with his eyes closed. Because of my strange notions about the power of beauty it never occurred to me that anyone would ever criticize him, no matter how he behaved. But here was another person, more beautiful perhaps than Asa.

My mother rubbed her forehead and then looked appraisingly at the stranger. She said to Asa, "Well, sweetheart, you know I always insist on the truth. I've never seen anyone like her. Except maybe in the movies.

"Are you an actress, Mrs. Higashi?"

"Oh, no. But my mother was an actress and singer."

My mother blushed again and turned to me. "Don't you think she's lovely, Joseph?" She turned back to look at Mrs. Higashi. "She has dark red hair, natural red, I can always tell, done up in a French twist. And she has green eyes. Just like emeralds. That means you can see clearly into her heart! And she's tall. Why don't you open your eyes, Asa? You really wouldn't want to miss seeing her." My mother giggled.

"Why are you laughing?" Asa said.

My mother addressed the stranger rather than Asa. "My late husband used to say, 'Tall women are the most beautiful.' That's why he fell in love with me." She put her hand near her mouth and whispered. "I used to be slender once, too."

I felt an unaccustomed embarrassment and annoyance with my mother, for which I was immediately ashamed. How could my heavy and plain-looking mother compare herself in any way, even if only in height, to the splendid creature standing in front of us. And why was she being so silly?

She said to Mrs. Higashi, "It's not often I meet a woman taller than me, or a man for that matter."

"Well, your husband was absolutely right. Certainly in your case. And my husband was of the same opinion. It's a great blessing to be tall. I do enjoy it."

Asa said, "What else does she look like?"

My mother looked at Mrs. Higashi. "Asa is very stubborn at times. I don't know what to do with him."

"I'm not stubborn."

Suddenly Eva Higashi crouched down so her face was almost level with Asa's. Her shimmering dress tightened over her hips, thighs, and breasts as she changed position. There was a faint whooshing sound. The slender heels of her blue-green shoes were suspended in the air. Only her toes were balanced on the ground.

She smiled and gently slipped off Asa's blindfold. He did not resist. His eyes were now wide open. He stared at her for a long time.

She had not appeared self-conscious or embarrassed by my mother's description nor was she now by Asa's scrutiny. She looked directly into Asa's eyes.

After a moment, Asa said very quietly, "She doesn't look Chinese."

"You mustn't say 'she' when the person is standing right in front of you," my mother said softly. "It's not polite, Asa. Talk to her directly. You heard her name. Mrs. Higashi."

"Are you from China, Mrs. Higashi?"

She laughed. "No, no. I lived in Japan for many years,

though I have been to China, too. My husband was Japanese. A doctor. Higashi is a Japanese name."

"Your husband is a doctor?" Asa asked.

"Yes. My husband was a children's doctor. He died last year. He was a wonderful man. He saved my life. Not too many women can say that about their husbands. I wish you could have met him. He always knew my heart." She smoothed Asa's hair with her hand. She spoke very solemnly. "If ever I remarry, though I don't intend to, I will keep the name of Higashi in his honor and blessed memory."

I wondered to myself what she would do if she did remarry and her new husband wanted her to use his name.

She turned her head and looked up at me, as if she had read my mind. "If I do remarry and my new husband wants me to use his name, I will have to call myself Eva Laquedem Higashi X—Laquedem being my maiden name, and X being my new husband's name, whatever it might be. Though as I said I don't intend to remarry any time soon and have no prospects at the moment."

She smiled as she said all this. She then stood up.

I noticed that when Eva Higashi said of her husband, "He always knew my heart," this touched my mother deeply. She was finding it difficult to maintain her composure. Finally my mother spoke, trying to sound cheerful. "You must think we're very impolite, Mrs. Higashi, asking you so many nosy questions."

"Not at all. You are kind people." She tapped her parasol on the floor. "I'm very delighted to be here."

"We are delighted, too," my mother said. "You're looking for a room, you said? We have one large and airy one upstairs. We call it the sunroom because it has so much light. It is very private. It even has its own bathroom and comes with full board and all house privileges. Would you like to come up and see it? We don't live in a mansion, it's just a simple home, and we are simple people, but I think you'll find it very comfortable."

Mrs. Higashi made a flourish with her hand. She spoke out loud as if she were after all an actress on a great stage:

"There was once a prince who stopped at a tiny, flimsy house adorned with white blossoms of Evening Faces. He asked himself: 'Who in this world has more than a temporary shelter? A hut, a jeweled pavilion, they are all the same.'"

She finished and bowed her head deeply.

My mother said, "Oh, that was lovely. And 'Evening Faces.' What a wonderful name for a flower. It must be Shakespeare. I forget which play. Did your mother perform Shakespeare?"

"Oh no, it is not Shakespeare. It's from an ancient novel written one thousand years ago by a noblewoman, Lady Murasaki. It's called *The Tale of Genji*."

None of us had heard of this novel or its author. It had never even occurred to us that there might be such things as Japanese novels.

"You must forgive us. We are so ignorant," my mother said. I was surprised by my mother's words. Although she had never been arrogant, my mother had always taken great pride in her knowledge of the Bible, which was the blue-print of the world. Now she was saying we were ignorant.

Eva Higashi smiled. "You must never say that. Never. There is so much in the world. How can one know every-thing? Even the wisest people may not know the most im-portant things. But I was lucky, my husband used to read to me from *Genji* very slowly, from a modern version, to teach me Japanese. In return I taught him the Bible. The language of the original *Genji* is very ancient and even the Japanese nowadays can't read it. It is filled with words whose mean-ing has been forgotten. My father once wrote an article on a similar phenomenon in the Bible, the hapax legomena, the words found only once."

" 'Ha-pax leg-o-me-na.' " My mother repeated each sylla-ble slowly. "I never heard that term. It sounds so interesting. Would you explain it more to me?"

"Of course. I would be happy to—"

"You speak Japanese?" Asa interrupted.

"*Hai!*" Mrs. Higashi said. "That means 'yes.' If you want I will teach you what I know. It is wonderful to know lan-guages. Learning a new language always cheers me up. My father spoke twelve. I only know a few."

"How many?" Asa asked.

"Seven."

I had never imagined this was even possible, I had such trouble just with Hebrew. I wondered, Where in the brain could one fit all those words?

Eva Higashi then made some more sounds that we'd never heard before.

She laughed. "That just means, 'It's a sunny day,' in Japanese!"

Asa said gravely, "The sun is destroying my eyes."

For a moment Eva looked puzzled. "But that cannot be true. The Bible says, 'The sun shall not harm you in the day nor the moon at night.' And so we have to have faith in that."

"Mrs. Higashi," my mother said, "you are so learned."

Mrs. Higashi just shook her head.

She then said to Asa, "Did you know I was related to the sun by marriage?"

We did not know what to say to this revelation. I saw a sudden look of confusion on my mother's face.

"Don't worry, I am not as crazy as I sound! Well, it is a strange story. My late husband came from a noble family. Just like Lady Murasaki. My husband was distantly related to the Emperor of Japan, and the Japanese believe the emperor is descended from the sun. So I suppose I am related by marriage. But despite my family connections, I love the moon and the stars more."

"The moon and the stars?" Asa asked.

"The moon is very mysterious and subtle. That's why poets prefer the moon. Are you a poet? I ask because you clearly have qualities of the moon."

"I do?"

"Yes. You are a very mysterious and subtle boy. But you would make a loyal friend, too, I think. The moon has been a great companion to me, as it is to every traveler, and a great comfort. One can always count on seeing the moon again and again wherever one goes."

"Not me. I'm going blind. I can't go outdoors. No matter what you say, I know the sun is destroying my eyes because a bad comet hit it."

"Asa has trouble seeing in the dark," my mother said.

Suddenly Mrs. Higashi stretched out both her arms and said, "Can you do what I do?"

Asa obeyed and stretched out his arms. He tried to do what she did.

She wiggled first this and then a different slender finger. She was testing his field of vision. Sometimes Asa wiggled his fingers back. Once or twice he didn't. She smiled the whole time as if he had done everything correctly. She kept saying "Bravo!"

"I met someone like you when I was in Siberia," she said, moving her right hand.

"You lived in Siberia?"

"No. I had to travel on the Trans-Siberian Railroad for eleven days to get to Vladivostok. Luckily it was summer in Siberia. Summer is very beautiful there and even hot! Most people don't realize that Siberia can be so hot. But it's better than being there in the winter. In the winter it's so cold your teeth can shatter like glass when you come indoors. Chik chuk." Mrs. Higashi tapped her front teeth with a red fingernail to emphasize her point. Her teeth were very white and even. "But I'm getting away from my story. On the train was a lovely little girl. She had a problem similar to yours. Her mother died before the journey so they asked me to pretend she was my daughter until we got to Vladivostok. She had red hair, too, so it was a perfect idea. We had to change her passport just a little so it would match mine."

"Vlad . . . Vladis . . ." Asa tried to say.

Eva Higashi slowly counted the syllables on her fingers. "Vla-di-vos-tok. On the edge of Russia! That's where we got the boat to Japan."

"Were the girl's eyes being destroyed by the sun?"

"Oh, no. That won't happen if you take the proper precautions.

"The little girl, Rachel, spent her time looking out the train window, storing up pictures for the future, so she could refer to them later, like Joseph in Egypt, laying up provisions for the lean years. Don't you think that was a clever idea?"

"Oh," Asa said. "Did she have to wear sunglasses?"

Mrs. Higashi thought for a moment. She glanced quickly at my mother, who was also waiting for the answer, her mouth slightly open.

"Oh yes, but she needed extra protection with the latitude of Siberia." She paused a moment. "Yes, now I remember. This is what we did. We made her a veil of transparent silk for going outdoors. Silk filters and softens sunlight. If you stop to think, it makes perfect sense since silkworms are very sensitive to light. It's a well-known fact. My husband's family owned a large silk mill but they lost everything in the war. Let me see if I have a piece." She opened her handbag. She reached in with her slender hand and shook out a pale blue square of material, thin as gossamer.

"Oh," my mother said. "It's silk veiling, isn't it?"

"This is the finest there is. I sometimes use silk to protect my hair. Let me show you what else we can do with it."

In a few deft movements Mrs. Higashi draped the scarf loosely around Asa's eyes so it hung like a veil. She tied the upper ends behind his head.

"Can you see through it?"

Asa looked around him. "Yes."

"But you still have to wear your sunglasses under it when you look outside, for double protection. Shall we test it and go to a window to look out?"

Asa put his sunglasses on under the silk veil. He followed her obediently to one of the windows. She pulled on the shade and it fluttered up.

The living room instantly brightened.

"Look. Does that outdoor light bother you now?"

Asa peered out at the front yard. "I don't think so."

"The silk will keep out any bad light, even from comets, so you won't have to worry indoors or out." She glanced at my mother. She said slowly, "Though as I said, when you go outside you must still wear your sunglasses. As soon as I am settled in we can go for a walk and try it out, that is, if it is all right for me to live here with you."

"Thank you," Asa said. "I don't know why the doctor never told me about this. He would have saved me a lot of trouble."

"Even the best doctors don't know everything. Nobody does. There's too much to know and too little time. I don't know everything either. I wasn't able to finish my studies,

though one day I will after I take care of some other important things. We mustn't get angry about our ignorance.
That's just the way it is."

Suddenly she loudly clapped her hands.

"Do you know how silkworms make silk?"

We were startled and did not know what to answer.

"Let me show you. Pay attention!"

Eva Higashi pulled two long silver pins out of her hair.
She lifted them above her head and slowly waved them together in the air, tracing a figure eight. She reminded me of
a hypnotist.

"The silkworm spins the silk from glands in its head
which it moves like this." She began to twist and gyrate.

"The silkworm uses up its own body to give its silk to us.
It shrinks while it spins its cocoon. Can you imagine a more
generous creature?"

We stood there mesmerized as Eva Higashi slowly
crouched down, shrinking like a silkworm. Her hands, still
holding the long silver pins, wove here and there, dancing
above her head and in front of her body.

While Eva moved, her red hair slowly loosened and
came apart. A wonderful fragrance was released as her hair
floated down over her face and shoulders, contrasting with
the blue-green of her dress. We could no longer see her face.

When she was finished, she put the pins in her mouth
and pulled her hair from her face and stood up again. She
began to gather her hair up over her head. She put both pins
in place. It seemed amazing to me that just two long pins

could hold up so much hair. When she was done, I noticed that at the head of each pin was the delicate figure of a bird.

"They're doves," she said, looking at us again. "Aren't they pretty?"

"They're lovely," my mother said.

"May we go up and see the room?"

"Of course," my mother said. "I hope you will like it."

CHAPTER 9

A S W E A P P R O A C H E D T H E S T A I R S,
Mrs. Higashi noticed my *tiykun*, which I'd
left lying open on the side table. Although
a moment before she seemed anxious to
go up and see the sunroom, she was dis-
tracted and stopped to pick it up.

She looked at it intently.

I said, "I was asked to be the new reader
in our synagogue, which is very hard to do.
Every week we read a portion of the Bible
in the synagogue and—"

"Oh, yes, of course," she said. She
smiled at me. "I'm sure you will do an excellent job."

Being interrupted, I felt that I had to

repeat my thought again from the beginning, then complete everything I originally intended to say. I needed to speak all the words and sentences together, in order. This impulse was new and alarming to me. I closed my eyes to get the words out before being interrupted again.

"I am the new reader in the synagogue, which is very hard to do. Every week we are supposed to read a portion in the synagogue. You have to be able to read it without seeing the vowels."

I opened my eyes. Mrs. Higashi was looking at me carefully. She smiled. I had a strange sensation. I was deeply moved though I did not understand why.

"Yes, you must keep everything together and in order, Joseph. That is very important. My father is the same way. That is how he became such a scholar, and you will be, too, one day, I'm sure. It takes a great deal of diligence to be a true scholar. I can see you have that quality. I'm so sorry I interrupted you. Yes, yes, the vowels are very important. The solid consonants are like our material bodies and the invisible vowels are like our souls that make our bodies come to life."

"What a wonderful way to put it," my mother said.

"A great rabbi once told that to my father."

Mrs. Higashi looked back in the *tiykun*. She skimmed across the column of the unvocalized text with a red fingernail.

"Look, it's already open to one of my favorite verses! I do not believe in coincidence. Do you?" She did not wait for us to answer and read in perfect Hebrew the words that Moses said to Joshua, "'*U'mi yitain kol am adonai n'vi'im . . .* Would that all God's people were prophets.'"

She looked up at us. "This is my father's favorite verse, too."

My mother timidly touched her on the arm. "It's so wonderful to have you in our house, Mrs. Higashi. Your father has taught you well. My own father taught me how to read the Bible. Please tell us about your father. Is he a rabbi?"

"Oh no, my father is not a rabbi." Mrs. Higashi smiled. "Though he knows more than any I've ever met. Many came to our house to learn from him. I always tried to listen to their discussions. But first, you really must call me Eva."

"Yes, Eva," my mother said. "But please tell us more about your father."

She paused and looked at each of us as if she were deciding whether she should continue, whether we were capable of understanding her.

She said, "I was very fortunate. My father tried to teach me as much as he could, though of course I only absorbed a fingertip of his vast knowledge." She held up one of her red nails with the fingers of her other hand. "I am an only child. My father always said, 'It is not enough to teach only boys and men. In these dark times everyone must carry as much knowledge within themselves as she can. That is the only way we have to save the past.'"

She suddenly appeared sad. "I've been away a long time and have forgotten so much. But not my father's words. I have not heard from him in years and cannot locate him. I'm afraid he is . . . No, no, I have not given up hope. You still hear stories about people who find each other again, even after many years."

For an instant she closed her eyes and shook her head slightly. She opened her eyes and now smiled brightly at us. "I know it sounds strange and so sudden. I am only here a few minutes, and this is a very different place from all the places I have ever been, but I feel I am safe at home again."

"Yes, Eva," my mother said. "Yes, Eva. This is your new home. Now let us finally show you your room."

CHAPTER 10

LTHOUGH MY MOTHER HAD HON-
estly said, "We don't live in a mansion,
it's just a simple home," the rooms in our
house were still very spacious with high
ceilings. Several months after my father
died and problems with money increased,
my mother had rearranged the large upstairs sunroom, where my father loved to
sit, to accommodate a boarder. This corner
room on the second floor of the house had
windows all along two of its walls, and
overlooked the backyard gardens.

The room was plainly but comfortably
furnished. There was a four-poster bed, a
writing desk, a small dark green love seat,
and a matching wing chair. The windows

were covered in a set of sheer curtains and a heavier set of drapes. Against one wall, between two large closets, stood an old-fashioned pier glass. On the remaining windowless wall were several fading watercolors of the Great Lakes.

Asa followed us up to the sunroom still wearing the silk that Eva had draped over his head. He looked all around and did not complain about the light streaming in from all the windows.

Eva walked around the room, touching the walls and window frames with her fingertips, glancing for a moment in the pier glass at herself and then us.

"Your wood moldings are so elegant. In Prague our whole apartment was paneled in mahogany. And we had a pretty view over the Vltava River from my father's study."

She walked over to a window and clapped her hands together.

"A view of your garden from my window! How lovely. And a sundial! Well, this is a little paradise."

"How did you get here?" Asa suddenly asked Eva. "Why did you come to us? Did you know our last tenant was an old man, Mr. Applewine? He died right here in this bed. But don't worry, my mother threw out the sheets. She changes them every week even though no one is sleeping in them. Sometimes when you die you make a mess."

"Asa!" my mother said but this did not stop him from talking.

"Dr. Fairclough came over and said Mr. Applewine died in his sleep of a heart attack. All the grown men in this house die but not the women. Iris May stayed a few days but she didn't die, which proves my point, so it will be safe for you." Asa was talking so rapidly he had to take in a deep breath.

"Asa, slow down," my mother said. "You'll choke on your words."

Asa asked again, "How did you get here? We're planning to go on an ocean liner someday soon. Mr. Zubrovsky and Iris May are on an ocean liner right now. That's why Joseph has to read the Torah. Did you come on an ocean liner from Japan, or did you fly on an airplane?"

"Asa, really, curiosity killed the cat," my mother said, but then she, too, turned expectantly to Eva Higashi.

Eva Higashi sat down on the end of the bed. She shifted her weight a few times to test if the mattress was comfortable. She seemed satisfied.

"It seems as if I've been traveling forever. Like the Wandering Jew who can never rest because of his sins, though I don't think I've done anything really bad. No, I don't think so. Not that I know of." She paused and smoothed the bedspread with her hands. "And I will tell you right now that I am a very poor sleeper. Anyway, little did I know when I left Japan that I would be sitting in this lovely room with such special people." She suddenly looked pained. "May I have some water? I am very thirsty."

"How awful of me. All this time and I didn't offer you anything," my mother said. "Joseph, will you run down and get a pitcher of water for Eva? Don't forget to put in ice."

I brought up a tray with a tall glass and a pitcher of ice water.

Eva said, "Thank you, Joseph." She poured herself a glass and brought it to her lips. She drank its contents in one long swallow. Eva then poured two more glassfuls, each time rapidly drinking the same way. She sat perfectly still for a moment, the now empty glass resting in her hand, waiting for the water to spread throughout her tall body. Small beads of perspiration appeared on her smooth forehead. Finally she said, "That was delightful. Thank you, Joseph."

Though she was the daughter of a scholar who wrote many articles and books, and she could quote the Bible even in Hebrew, I noticed that she did not say a blessing before drinking the water. Perhaps she was so thirsty she forgot.

Finally Asa asked a third time, "How did you get here? Did you come on an ocean liner?"

Eva turned to Asa. "Yes, yes, as a matter of fact I did come to America on an ocean liner."

CHAPTER 11

SEVERAL WEEKS BEFORE SHE AR-
rived in Windsor, Eva set sail from Yoko-
hama to San Francisco on the passenger
freighter *Jewel of the Seas*. From the port-
holes of her small cabin and from the rails
of the narrow promenade deck, she looked
back on the grandeur of Mount Fuji as the
ship slowly entered Sagami Bay.

It was an unusually clear day. In the
morning light, the volcano's base appeared
dark green from the trees growing on its
lower slopes. Its cone, rising into the
clouds, was dark red. As the afternoon approached, the entire mountain turned pale
violet.

"Mount Fuji is sacred to the Japanese," Eva told us.

She took a moment from her story and asked for a pen and piece of paper. She showed us how the Japanese make the pictograph for volcano. We learned that "volcano" is composed of two different symbols.

"See, this is the symbol for fire— 火. See the little flames? And this is the one for mountain— 山. See the soaring peaks? Together they mean 'volcano.'"

"Can I try drawing it?" Asa asked.

"Yes, of course."

Asa carefully copied the pictograph.

"That's perfect, Asa," Eva said.

She continued her story.

The first evening at sea, the captain of the *Jewel of the Seas* invited Eva to his dinner table. He wrote an invitation on his own fine stationery and had it delivered in the afternoon by one of his stewards. He addressed Eva respectfully by her name as it appeared on the ship's registry, Mrs. Chujo Higashi of Fukuoka Prefecture. He also invited another passenger, the only other woman on the ship, the delicate and frail-looking Mrs. Miyashita. Eva had seen Mrs. Miyashita that first morning, sitting on a deck chair, looking at photographs and letters she kept in a lacquerware box.

It was a charming evening. The waters of the Pacific were calm. The food was excellent.

Mrs. Miyashita told everyone that she was going to join her daughter in California. She showed everyone Akiko's picture.

"She's very beautiful," Eva said.

The captain agreed.

Eva then told the others that after a long wait in receiving her visa, she was moving to America. She would first do some exploring before deciding exactly where she would settle.

Maybe she would end up in New York City. She had grown up in a cosmopolitan city, so she might like living there. Sadly, she told the captain and Mrs. Miyashita, she could not return to her homeland with the political situation there. Everyone agreed that nowadays the situation everywhere was certainly very complicated.

The captain asked Eva about her itinerary in America.

After she told him he said, "You will be traveling in a great zigzag!"

Eva laughed. "Really? Well, I suppose that will be more interesting than traveling in a straight line."

"That's true," he agreed.

They then talked of places they had been and all the people and events they had witnessed. As if by silent agreement, they tried to speak only of happy times.

Mrs. Miyashita had traveled widely in her youth. She had even spent a year in Paris studying to be a painter, although she quickly added that she had no real talent. While in France she had met the artist Claude Monet. She told Eva and the captain about the influence that Japanese art had on this great painter, and this led to a discussion of ukiyo-e prints. Eva did not believe in simple coincidence. As it turned out, in her trunk Eva carried nine of these color woodblock prints from the *Fugaku sanjū-rokkei* series, the *Thirty-six Views of Mount Fuji* by the nineteenth-century artist Hokusai. Eva told the captain and Mrs. Miyashita how she had received these gifts from her late husband's family.

"My dear husband has recently died. He was sick a very long time." Then she added quietly, "He was near the radiation."

"I'm very sorry to hear about your husband," the captain said.

Mrs. Miyashita lightly touched Eva's hand with the edge of her folded fan. Her own husband had died many years before, when Akiko was a little girl.

"I did not mean to talk of sad things," Eva said. "At least we were happy to be together, even when my husband was already sick."

Mrs. Miyashita then revealed that she once had several ukiyo-e prints herself, and several ancient and very valuable silk scrolls from the Muromachi period in the late fourteenth century. They were all destroyed when her home in Tokyo burned down. Luckily she had been visiting at her sister's summerhouse in the mountain resort of Karuizawa when the fire-bombing occurred. Otherwise she, too, would have been killed. The memory made her cry and her heavily applied makeup began to smudge around her eyes.

"Forgive me for retreating into sadness during such a happy evening." She excused herself from the table.

Eva and the captain both got up to help her.

"No, no. I will be all right," Mrs. Miyashita said, and left the dining room alone.

THE NEXT MORNING on the promenade deck, Eva offered Mrs. Miyashita one of her prints, a view of Fuji from the Nihonbashi Bridge in Edo.

"Oh, Mrs. Higashi. I could never accept such an extravagant gift."

"Please do. I have so many. I can do without one," she said.

Mrs. Miyashita said, "You are very kind, but I could never take such a treasure from you. Besides it was a gift from your husband's family. You must keep them all. What has happened to me is over now. I must not look back at the past. I was wrong to be so upset. It is wrong to cry over material things."

For several days as they made their way across the Pacific, Eva continued to urge Mrs. Miyashita to take the Hokusai print. Finally one morning she relented. "I will always be grateful for your kindness."

"No, it is you who have done me a kindness by accepting my small gift."

That evening Mrs. Miyashita knocked on Eva's cabin door. She bowed and presented Eva with a package wrapped in brightly colored paper. Inside Eva found the lacquerware box, nine or ten inches square, the same box in which Mrs. Miyashita had kept her photographs and letters. Now holding it in her hands, Eva saw the elegant painting on the cover, a woman in Chinese dress looking toward the horizon.

Mrs. Miyashita explained: "It's a scene from the story of

Lady Wenji. Do you know it, Mrs. Higashi? She was kidnapped by the Xiongu Mongols and given to their chieftain as a wife." Mrs. Miyashita touched her delicate finger to the lid. "Here Lady Wenji is thinking of her family far away in China."

"It's so lovely," Eva said. "Your daughter must be thinking of you the same way, with great longing."

Mrs. Miyashita began to cry.

Eva was alarmed. "I'm sorry. My words have upset you again."

"No, no, of course not, it is my own fault. My emotions have become most fragile and uncontrollable."

Mrs. Miyashita then admitted that she did not know where her daughter Akiko lived. She could be living anywhere. America was such an enormous country, if she was even still there.

Before the war, her daughter had received several letters from Boston. She would not let her mother see them. Perhaps, Mrs. Miyashita thought, she had a suitor there. Perhaps she went to Boston to meet him. Akiko had always been secretive and stubborn, going out evenings all by herself, meeting foreign men. It was not correct behavior and it had led to this. One morning before the war broke out, Mrs. Miyashita found her daughter's room empty. And now, all this time later, Mrs. Miyashita had still not heard from her.

Mrs. Miyashita had friends in several American cities with whom she herself could stay, but what could they do to find her daughter? It was like finding a needle in a haystack. Her journey, she knew, was completely senseless. It was doomed to failure. Still, she could not help herself. She had to go. She did not want to die without seeing her daughter one more time.

"I do not know what I will find in America. Even if a miracle happens and I find my daughter, I do not know if she will speak to me."

"Perhaps when she realizes you have traveled across the world to find her she will rejoice in seeing you. She will always be your daughter, after all."

FROM SAN FRANCISCO Eva journeyed to Los Angeles, and from there to Denver. From Denver she journeyed to Houston, from Houston to Minneapolis, from Minneapolis to New Orleans, and from New Orleans to Chicago. They were amazing cities, large and sprawling and energetic. Their people were always friendly but she still did not feel at home in any of them. She did not sleep well the entire time though she stayed in fine hotels.

Although Eva had never been in the United States before and did not know anybody there personally, there were people who knew of her.

When she arrived in Chicago and settled in her hotel, she received an express letter.

Dear Miss Laquedem:

It has come to my attention that you had been living in Japan and have recently been traveling in the

United States. I hope you may have retained in your
possession the Augsburg Miscellany *that has been in*
your father's family for generations. This manuscript is
of great interest to me. I already have in my collection
three other works by the same scribe and illustrator
who, as the daughter of a great scholar no doubt
knows, executed several commissions for the trusted
factotum of the Fugger banking family, the wealthy Jew
Solomon De Braga. Would you kindly consider meeting
me in Detroit at your earliest convenience? I regret that
frailty prevents me from traveling even the short dis-
tance to Chicago and that old age has made me so
importunate.

Yours sincerely,
Prof. Xavier I. Hirschmann
Dealer in Rare Books and Manuscripts
Pontiac, Michigan

The *Augsburg Miscellany,* Eva explained to us, had indeed been in the Laquedem family for many generations
even as they migrated from place to place in Christian Europe, the Ottoman Empire, and back.

As with many important and rare manuscripts, Eva was
aware that there were people in the world who had long
known this information. Still she had taken the manuscript
in utmost secrecy and had told no one about it besides her
husband, Chujo.

Perhaps Professor Hirschmann knew her father, even if

she could not recall her father mentioning Hirschmann's name. Perhaps the professor knew what had happened to her father.

"And so, you understand, I had to come to Detroit and see who this person was."

She thought she might also enjoy seeing other examples in Professor Hirschmann's collection of the great illuminator her father's family had treasured and protected for so many generations. Her father had often told her how one of the originally conceived illuminations in the miscellany had inspired his consuming interest in the world of the Bible. As a boy he had become enchanted by a depiction of the Pillar of Cloud leading the camp of Israel away from Pharaoh's army. Atop the towering figure of the cloud, the artist managed to evoke the image of a kindly face in shades of gray and white tempera flecked with gold. Her father claimed that it was this childhood discovery which years later resulted in his article "Ursprung und Wanderschaften der übernatürlichen Wolken durch die Wüste und uralte Literatur," and later still his unfinished book, *Clouds of Glory*.

From Chicago she traveled to Detroit, where she stayed downtown at the Statler Hotel on Washington Boulevard.

The porters who carried her gray trunk placed it in the center of the room, on an orange Chinese carpet woven with intertwined dragons.

The porters pointed out the window to the panoramic view.

"There, lady, you can see Canada!"

She noted the position of the afternoon sun. "Canada? But aren't we facing south?"

They looked at each other and laughed. "Well, ma'am, that's where Canada is!" They explained to her how the peninsula of southwestern Ontario reached down between the Great Lakes.

Later that day, Professor Hirschmann, a frail old man with thin gray hair, came to her suite. He was accompanied by a nurse, a stocky woman in uniform. The nurse said nothing, and Professor Hirschmann did not introduce her.

"The nurse stared at me," Eva told us. "She was most fearsome."

Professor Hirschmann sat down on a small love seat.

Unlike his nurse, Professor Hirschmann was friendly, at least at first. He was clearly a man of great learning and culture. He told her how he had been ordained a minister and was a member of the theological faculty at the University of Berlin. Like Eva's father, he was an expert in ancient languages and literature, Hebrew, Akkadian, Aramaic, and Eblaite. He had suffered much in the war. His house in the Charlottenburg district of Berlin was bombed and his wife, Elise, and their dog, Bobo, were killed. These tragedies accounted for his appearance beyond his years and for his frailty.

Professor Hirschmann was able to save his own collection of Hebrew manuscripts, which he kept hidden at his country house and brought with him when he left for the United States after the war. Collecting was his only remaining and constant pleasure. The only other constant in his life was—he whispered to Eva in Hebrew—*hamachashefa shama*—"that witch over there," nodding ever so slightly in the direction of his nurse, who apparently did not understand this language.

Eva offered to call room service. Did the Herr Professor want something to drink or to eat?

"Gnädige Frau, that is very kind of you but I have a kitchen and a cook at home." She noticed how even when he smiled the corners of his mouth were turned down slightly. Eva pulled at the corners of her own mouth to demonstrate this to us. We laughed.

"Oh, but I didn't mean to make you laugh," Eva said very seriously. "That's exactly how he looked. It was very strange. I thought it was because he had suffered so much."

She continued her story.

Professor Hirschmann said to her, "As you can see, young Miss Laquedem, I'm a man on the edge of the world and time. For me the collection of manuscripts is an addiction. Have I guessed correctly? You have it? May I see what I have long desired to see?"

She brought the manuscript out to him. She handed him a pair of white gloves. He looked at them as if in great pain. "One can tell so much more from touching the parchment itself," he said. Nevertheless he put the gloves on.

He looked over the *Augsburg Miscellany*, turning its pages slowly.

Tears came to his eyes. He was careful to wipe them

with his handkerchief so as not to allow them to fall on the ancient pages.

"It is the most beautiful thing I have ever seen."

While he was inspecting the manuscript, she asked him: Had he ever met her father? Perhaps in Berlin or in Prague? Her father had attended universities in Vienna and Berlin, and after his studies were complete, he often traveled to Germany and Austria to lecture.

"Yes, yes. I saw your father a long time ago. I heard him speak in Berlin. I do not remember exactly where or when. I have never been to Prague. But as you know it was no secret that your father's family had such a wonderful treasure."

She asked more questions:

"How did you acquire the other manuscripts out of Augsburg? Were they in your family?" She did not know that any other manuscripts existed besides two—she had never seen them herself—which were privately owned by wealthy families. For a moment she was uncertain of these families' names. Were they the Feldspeisers and the Obermeyers? The Feldspeisers had become Christians.

"Perhaps the honored professor's mother was a Feldspeiser."

"My mother was certainly not a Feldspeiser," Professor Hirschmann said. "In times of upheaval, young lady, everything becomes available. People are always needing money. There are people who would sell their children and parents for money."

"How awful. What do you mean?"

He smiled. "Excuse me, I was being too harsh. We have all lived through difficult times."

"How did you know I was coming to America? And that I had the *Augsburg Miscellany* with me?"

"I did not even know you existed until recently. But when I found out, I assumed your father would have given you his greatest treasure for safekeeping. It was the quite obvious thing to do. I was correct, wasn't I?"

"How did you find out about me?"

"How? I am a collector. And collectors do not give away their trade secrets. But it is not hard to find people if you try."

He then looked at her straight in the eyes.

His tongue, a sickly gray digit, flickered a moment over his lower lip.

"Miss Laquedem, let me come to the point. You may disagree with my behavior and find it unfitting for a man of my station. The Bible says you shall not covet, but I do. It is a very great sin and can lead to all sorts of others. Judge me as you will. I cannot help myself. That is the type of person I am. But I think you will agree that seventy-five thousand dollars can go a long way in this childlike country."

It took her a moment to realize that he was making an extraordinary offer for the *Augsburg Miscellany*.

"Well, what do you have to say?"

She was astonished. She knew the *Augsburg Miscellany* was a masterpiece of historical and artistic value but she had never expected such a figure nor had she ever considered parting with this family treasure for the sake of money. It had been in her family for so many generations. She confessed to us that she was tempted. Protecting the miscellany all this time in uncertain circumstances had been a terrible burden. Surely someone who was willing to spend so much money to buy it would do everything to protect it.

She did not know what to do.

She could not speak.

"I see. As I guessed. You drive a hard bargain. Then I will give you one hundred thousand American dollars. Cash. That is as far as I will go. For that money you can live like a queen."

She nodded.

"Good. Then we are agreed." The old man rose and walked with crablike movements to the secretaire. He leaned his mahogany cane against its side and motioned to the nurse, who, Eva now realized, was carrying a briefcase.

Eva felt light-headed.

The face of her father appeared before her. It hovered just outside the window of her Statler Hotel suite, where just before she had seen Canada.

"Oh, Father!"

"What did you say?" the old man asked.

"Nothing."

It was just like in the famous Midrash of Joseph and Potiphar's Wife, Eva told us.

"And Joseph entered the house to do his work," the Bible said, and the Midrash explained: The image of Jacob, Joseph's father, came to him at a window to stop him from committing adultery with Potiphar's Wife.

Now, at the Statler Hotel in Detroit, when Eva tried to

look again at old Professor Hirschmann seducing her with money, her father's face appeared first at the window. Then her father's countenance came into the suite. Now it hovered between Eva and Professor Hirschmann above the Chinese carpet.

Her father had been crying.

He shook his head slowly and disappeared.

Eva understood. She had almost made a terrible mistake and let greed rule her. After all, she had every material thing she needed in this world.

"I'm sorry," she said, trembling. "I cannot sell it. I am sorry you have taken so much trouble."

"But I am prepared to pay you cash. You might need that. You are accustomed to the good things in life." He glared at his nurse. "Elfride!" The nurse came over and slammed the briefcase on the secretaire. He opened it. It was packed full of American bills.

He leered at Eva. "Don't you like the smell?"

"I'm sorry. The *Augsburg Miscellany* is not for sale."

He thumped his ebony cane on the carpet, striking the blue head of a dragon. The top of the cane, she suddenly noticed, was the head of a man, with exaggerated features, long rabbit ears and a beaklike nose.

Professor Hirschmann raised his voice.

"Who do you think you are? How dare you back out on the deal we just made! I will not pay another cent! You are grasping like all your people! Who else would be willing to pay such an outrageous sum!"

"'Grasping'?" she repeated in barely a whisper. "'Outrageous sum'? There is nothing for sale here, Herr Professor. There never was. I am sorry for your misunderstanding."

She pointed to the door.

At first he did not move.

She went to the telephone to call the concierge.

He then moved toward the door and glared at her. "I found you once and I will find you again. I know you and what you are. I will not be patient much longer. You cannot hold out forever."

He shouted at his nurse, who had been staring at the money in the briefcase wide-eyed. *"Elfride! Komm!"* The nurse stood there a moment. She now glared at Eva.

The old man yelled at his nurse again, *"Elfride! Hör zu! Komm! Komm!"* He shut the briefcase and picked it up off the secretaire. His nurse followed him as he made his way to the door. The nurse made no effort to help him.

Minutes later, from the window of her hotel suite, Eva looked down twenty floors to the street. She was shaking. She knew she had almost done something terrible.

"Otherwise why would my father have come to me?" she asked us.

Emerging from under the entrance canopy of the Statler Hotel, the old man was now an insect figure brandishing a cane.

A limousine was parked on Washington Boulevard. A man in livery opened the door and the old man crept in. The car sped away.

Eva stood at the window a long time.

After she had calmed herself, she looked up and across the river and saw what suddenly seemed the most tranquil city on earth. The delightful scene in the distance, the orderly tree-lined streets and rows of kindly houses soothed her.

Perhaps tomorrow she would go there and do some sightseeing. Yes, it would do her good. She was exhausted and went to bed early, unpacking only what she needed for the night. Although she suffered terribly from insomnia and had not slept well in weeks, that night she fell into a deep and dreamless slumber.

S O N O W I A M H E R E W I T H Y O U, what with the foolish misunderstanding about my visa. It's hard to believe so much has happened to me and changed in one day."

My mother said, "You were brought to us for a reason, Eva. God has His reasons for everything even if we don't understand them."

Eva brought her hand up to her chin as if she were hearing the most amazing pronouncement from my mother. The ruby bracelet she had bought that morning from Greta Feld sparkled.

Eva said, "You are kind, Adele. I am grateful to you. God will surely reward you."

"He already has, Eva. He already has," my mother said. "Just look at me sitting here. Just look at my two treasures."

"Yes, I see. I see." She thought a moment and then she said, "Well, now it's time to show you one of mine. I've just been talking about it and it is in some way responsible for my being here with you."

Eva opened her large handbag. She took out a pair of white cotton gloves and put them on slowly. Her fingers were long and slender. She smiled at us, as if we were in some sort of delightful conspiracy together. She reached again into her handbag, this time taking out a lacquerware box, the one Mrs. Miyashita had given her on the *Jewel of the Seas*. She placed it gently on the bed.

She opened the box and removed a rectangular leather case embossed with gold. At each corner was a small pearl, one of which she touched for a moment, stroking it ever so lightly.

Asa and I were sitting on either side of Eva. My mother sat facing us all on a chair. We all leaned anxiously toward the wonderful object in Eva's hands.

Asa said, "What is it? Let me see."

"Look while I hold it. We must be careful, it is almost five hundred years old. Only I may touch it. That's my only request."

She suddenly appeared nervous. She looked around her, although there was no one but us in the room.

"There is one more request that I must make, though I have told you so much already. For many years, until my foolish meeting yesterday, I have been careful not to speak of this. It has been very difficult having no one to talk to since my husband died. This must be our secret. It is a great treasure. I have risked my life for it. If anyone finds out they might try to take it from me. Do you understand? That is why I always keep it with me. Will you promise me?"

My mother said, "We promise, Eva. Please do not worry." My mother turned to us. "Do you understand, boys? This is very serious. Please promise Eva."

Asa and I promised.

Eva smiled in relief. "Oh, thank you."

She turned her attention back to the object in her hands. She flipped open a small gold clasp and the case opened into a book.

Carefully, Eva turned the pages until she came to the place she was looking for.

Delicately, she pointed to the words on the right-hand page. They were from Psalm 104:

> *Zeh hayom—Here is the sea great and wide,*
> *wherein are creeping things without number,*
> *small creatures and great!*

She pointed to a miniature painting that filled the opposite page. It was an ocean scene in brilliant blue. She tilted the book to catch the light.

"Let me see!" Asa cried.

"Just one moment." Eva rested the book on her lap. "The

illuminations were done small. It is best to look at them with this." From her handbag she took out a large magnifying glass and handed it first to Asa.

"See, when you look closely, how the water is swarming with life?"

Asa said, "They're swimming under the water!"

It was true. Shimmering beneath the surface of a lapis lazuli sea were pale sapphire forms of fish—all kinds—and dolphins.

Never had I beheld anything so exquisite. I felt my heart beat faster.

My mother said, "I've never seen anything like this, Eva."

"Who is that?" Asa asked. On the opposite page, he pointed to a figure of a slender youth who seemed oddly familiar. Eva very gently prevented Asa's finger from touching the parchment.

"That is Alexander of Augsburg, the artist and scribe. He put himself in all his works. See how he gestures and points, as if he were escorting us through the words, as if he were beckoning us to enter his private world. He is pointing to that great whale over there, the Leviathan!

"Alexander was very handsome, don't you agree? He drew himself as a boy although he was already an older man when he made this book. It took him ten years to copy all the texts and to illustrate them, more time than I lived in Japan! Though when I was in Japan, I did not accomplish very much, I am ashamed to say. My father said the miscellany was Alexander's greatest work. I myself never saw another to compare."

Eva turned her head abruptly. "Why, he looks a little like you, Asa!"

"He does?"

"I think so. What do you think?" Eva asked my mother and me.

It upset me to realize Eva was right. Alexander of Augsburg did look like Asa with his fair hair, fine features, and slender limbs. I could not help thinking, Perhaps she will think that Asa is as great as Alexander of Augsburg. Even though Asa drew so well, how could he be as great as Alexander of Augsburg? And Asa had terrible handwriting.

"See how he's dressed?" Eva pointed. "Sometimes he drew himself in the clothes of different lands. He traveled all over the world, even as far as India. Here he is in a Venetian sailor's outfit.

"Let me show you something else," she said. She turned to the back of the miscellany. She showed us a strange and colorful design, the colophon, or emblem, of Alexander of Augsburg.

The aleph—**א**, the four-limbed, headless letter that initiated and represented his name—was drawn large, almost a quarter of the page, transfigured into a strange bird, its two eagle-clawed feet on the ground, its upper extremities gilded wings, folded forward, protecting itself.

Below it was written, "I, Alexander of Augsburg, wrote and illuminated this book for ten years in the palace of Solomon De Braga and completed it in the year of Creation 5233."

This I quickly calculated was equivalent to the secular year 1473.

"That is correct, Joseph," Eva said.

"What does the bird symbolize?" my mother asked Eva. "His name has nothing to do with birds, does it?"

"Perhaps they are the wings of the Divine Presence, the holy Shekhinah, or the wings of eagles which will carry God's people back to Jerusalem when the Messiah comes."

"What a lovely idea," my mother said.

"Yes, it is. Now I will put everything away. We will look at it again another time."

Eva gently closed the miscellany. She put it back in the lacquerware box, which she left on the bedspread.

For a moment we were all quiet. Finally we could not help asking, Didn't she love this amazing treasure she was so fortunate to own? Would she really have been ready to part with it even if her father's face had not appeared to her in the suite at the Statler Hotel?

Had she really been tempted by money?

But she said to us laughing, "Well, one hundred thousand dollars cash is a great deal of money!"

My mother laughed, too. "It's a fortune! I would be so nervous if I had to carry such a valuable thing with me!"

Eva said, "I worry every minute, Adele. Sometimes it is overwhelming. I have a great responsibility." She then continued, now trying to answer our other questions.

She had, after all, already enjoyed the manuscript for many years. It had given her great solace and strength on her long journeys just as the moon had. But as precious and dear as any object was, she emphasized, moving her hands through the air as if she were molding the light, it was only a thing. Perhaps, like all material things, the miscellany was only an illusion.

"Even if I did not have it anymore in my possession I would always own it because I owned it once."

"What do you mean, Eva?" Asa asked.

"Anything you have ever seen or heard or held in your hands changes you. It becomes a part of you. It's a scientific fact. Your brain changes. Why, when we look at each other right now, we are being changed forever. We are becoming part of each other."

We looked at each other but did not notice any change.

"Well, in any case, you are certainly right. I was wrong even to think of selling the miscellany, as my father let me know. Great harm may have come to it had it gotten into the wrong hands. I have the duty to protect it. That is much more important than owning it."

"What happened to your father?" Asa asked. "Is he coming here, too?"

"I do not know what happened to my father after I left Prague. I received one letter from him and then nothing more. I'm afraid he was taken away to some horrible place. No one has heard from him again. I am afraid he may be dead."

"Why don't you go to Prague and look for him?" Asa asked. "Maybe he's in your apartment."

"I can't, Asa. It could be dangerous. Everything has changed. They might even try to take the miscellany from me. I would not be allowed to keep such a treasure. No. If my father were alive I would have heard from him. Someone would have told me."

"But your father must be okay if he came to visit you in the hotel," Asa said.

"That's so kind of you to say, Asa. Maybe you are right. I will try contacting people again. I have tried so many times and failed. Maybe someone has gotten more recent news."

Eva rose from the bed. She walked back and forth before us in that same way she had entered the house, as if she were moving between her world and ours. Her smile was not directed at any of us. Her ways, I realized, were different from ours. She came from a different world, and I realized she must be very upset despite her smile. Perhaps we had upset her with our questions. I had the strange notion that she and the unknown world she came from were more real than we were. She seemed more alive, in her blue-green silk dress, which rustled softly, than any of us.

She moved into a shaft of sunlight. The light at her feet made the floor disappear. She hovered there, tall and weightless. And we who were so dull and ignorant, who had never before heard of Japanese novels, or how silkworms made silk from their very own bodies, or that the brain changes when we look upon each other, we sat heavily in our shadowy seats.

She began to ask us questions in return:

Did anything belong to us forever?

Did we own even ourselves, the very bodies in which we reside and move through the world, and which could be taken from us at any time? Wasn't the moment of death concealed from us as the famous Midrash had asked and answered? She quoted it for us:

"'Where is the Day of Death? The Day of Death is hidden, but the Holy One Blessed be He and His ministering angels hold the days of our lives in their hands.'"

She asked us: "If we could not own even ourselves, how could a person own another thing?"

She answered her own question.

"Only God can own things. As King David said, 'To God belongs the earth and all that is in it.' This world does not belong to us. We are only here to help care for it."

None of us knew what to say. Although he was only a child, her words upset Asa greatly.

"Don't cry," my mother said to Asa, but she began crying softly, too.

Eva took Asa's hand and said to him, "Now, now, it's nothing to cry about. I did not mean to upset you. I am very sorry. I should not have spoken of such things." She turned to my mother. "Please forgive me, Adele. I did not mean to upset Asa or you. I should not have spoken of these things in front of your children. It is a terrible way for me to repay your kindness. Please, will you forgive me?"

"I am not upset with you, Eva. What you're saying is true. My boys are not too young to hear the truth. I never hide it from them. I just never thought about the things you said."

Eva then spoke very softly to Asa, almost in a whisper. It was hard for me to hear her.

"We all own something more important, our souls, which are more important than our human bodies and our senses. No one can ever take your soul away from you. Your soul is forever. Everything else is for a very short while. The secret is not to care too much for all those other things you cannot keep. I have lost so many things in my life, many precious things. I am always losing something, it seems, but I can still be happy because I know I will always exist somehow. Just as I know my father exists somewhere because he came to me yesterday in the hotel.

"I had not seen my father in ten years. Not even in a dream."

I could not help thinking as I watched Eva whispering these words to Asa, This woman is so beautiful, that is why things have been hard for her. That is why she is always losing so much.

At the same time I was overwhelmed by her ideas, which were new and strange to me.

Back then, when I first heard them, I felt a great if temporary relief, as if all my worries and crazy thoughts were melting away. For if the things this stranger was saying were true, there was no reason to ever feel bad or be unhappy despite all the sad things that happen in the world.

Even now, all these years later, I have held on to those words. I have tried to write about them in my own way, preserving them in my little book even though they still seem new and strange to me.

Perhaps, whether these ideas are true or foolish, they

have helped save me from myself. I cannot say I have ac-
cepted them fully, but I have tried as hard as I could to nur-
ture my soul as if it might already exist somehow in a
separate immortal realm. I never speculate on what this soul
consists of. I would not dare. It seems to me oddly beside the
point. We cannot see or perceive it.

"Sometimes I see my father, too," Asa said to Eva.
"Though I don't remember him too well." He stopped crying and wiped his eyes.

Eva said, "I knew you would understand me."

Eva then picked up the lacquerware box from the bedspread.

Her voice brightened.

"I will put this away now. We will look at it again another
time soon. It is very old and must be treated with great care.
In return it can give us much pleasure. I am sorry I let Professor Hirschmann hold it for so long. I should have never
let him touch it. I feel I owe it an apology."

LATE THAT AFTERNOON, Eva Higashi and my
mother returned from customs. Two men from the Statler
Hotel carried her large trunk into our house and up to her
room.

In Eva's wallet was a wad of American money, and from
it she settled her hotel account. She then gave each of the
men an extra bill.

"Oh, thank you, lady," they said.

When they left, Eva turned to my mother. "Let me pay you for the first month." She offered my mother a small pile of bills.

"Wait, Eva," my mother said. "Wait until next week. We will start counting next week. This week is almost over and you will be our guest."

THAT FIRST EVENING Eva would not eat dinner with us.

"But you must be hungry, Eva," my mother said. "You have had such a long day."

"Oh, no, I have so much to do to settle in. Don't worry about me. I'm never hungry when I'm busy. Perhaps I can have just a piece of cheese and toast. I shall eat that in my room, if it is all right."

"Of course, Eva."

"Are there any mice? I am very afraid of mice."

My mother laughed. "Oh, no. They are not permitted in Canada!"

"Really? We did not have mice in our apartment in Prague, but I saw them once in Japan."

That evening I read through the *parsha* three times. I was ready to read it through a fourth time but my head began to ache and I could not practice any more.

I went outdoors alone. I stood in the backyard and looked up. Through the drawn curtains I saw Eva's shadow moving purposefully through her lighted room as she unpacked her trunk. She moved back and forth, holding in her hands objects that I could not quite make out, mysterious undulating forms that were projected with her shadow on the curtains.

I looked around me and saw more fireflies in our yard than I had ever seen before. Perhaps they flew and gathered themselves here from the whole neighborhood. Perhaps they were as inquisitive as I, strangely attracted to the lanternlike glow of her room.

I WAS EXHAUSTED and went to bed early. I was so tired I forgot to check the cutlery in the kitchen drawers. When I realized this omission, I was already lying in my bed. I did not even care. It was a great relief for me not to care. What could it possibly matter if the knives, spoons, and forks were stacked perfectly? They were only material things and of no lasting importance. What effect could they have on my life or my soul, which would exist forever?

I dreamed of Eva's father, who, in my imagination, was like the fading memories I had of my own father. Emaciated, Enoch Laquedem sat in the paneled library of the apartment on Pařížká Street. The library was filled with the most wonderful brilliance.

Asa sat with Eva's father, looking into one of his books, moving his small index finger across the pages.

They were reading from a book of Midrashim.

"Yes, yes," Eva's father said. "Here it is. I found it. The famous Midrash on Evening Faces! Let us read it together."

I read along with them from this ancient Hebrew commentary on Evening Faces. Somehow I was reading with Asa's eyes. The commentary began with the sacred verses, "Who in this world has more than a temporary shelter? A hut, a jeweled pavilion, they are all the same."

From this starting point the dream Midrash went on to explain the meaning of the Evening Faces that Prince Genji saw, the deep mysteries and great truths to be found in their fragrant countenances, and how we and everything in the world were bound up in them. What the Midrash explained seemed compelling beyond measure, for as another verse in that dream confirmed, God joined in the Evening Faces two holy attributes: wisdom and beauty.

Suddenly, while all was being revealed, I heard my father's voice calling to me.

Asa looked up in surprise. The book of Midrashim with its profound explanations disappeared from my view. There were now two holes where Asa's eyes should have been and I could see straight through the back of his head.

I was terrified and awoke. In those confused and vanishing moments, I could no longer remember anything of the deep mysteries and great truths that had just been revealed to me so vividly. I was angry with my father for causing Asa to look up in the dream, but my foolish anger quickly faded. How could I be angry with my poor dead father? It was only a dream.

Though I knew then that this lost revelation of the Evening Faces may have been an illusion, when I think of it all these years later I am still filled with a sense of loss and sorrow.

CHAPTER 13

URING MY LONG SCIENTIFIC career I have traveled extensively. I have lectured at numerous international scientific congresses in my own field of human and comparative neuroanatomy as well as at those of the related disciplines of neurosurgery, neurology, and neuroscience. I find this interdisciplinary interest gratifying. I often find the divisions within the sciences, and even between the sciences and humanities, artificial, an artifact of the vast accumulation of human knowledge. There is too much to know and so we divide things up to absorb them.

From time to time over the years I have been invited as a visiting professor to vari-

ous universities and institutions throughout the world.
These stays have ranged from several weeks to almost a year
and have provided opportunities for me, not only to teach
others what I have painstakingly discovered, but to learn
what is happening elsewhere in the scientific universe.

Wherever I have gone, I have used the occasion to
broaden myself in still other ways, by visiting local libraries
and museums that might have Hebrew manuscripts in their
collections. I have even chosen certain conferences and professorships based solely on the proximity of an interesting
collection.

In my pursuit of knowledge in this rarified field, I have
not confined myself to the rarest or most famous or most
luxurious manuscripts but have included even the modest.
When possible I have also studied manuscripts from other
cultures: Christian, Islamic, Persian. In Kyoto, where I spent
a research year, I was able to visit many temple and museum
libraries. I saw many exquisite calligraphy works on silk and
paper scrolls spanning almost a millennium.

I have learned the enormous value of parallel inquiry
from the field of comparative neuroanatomy and have applied it to my study of manuscripts. Even seemingly unrelated creatures teach about each other and about our
human selves. The understanding of our visual systems has
been broadened by the study not only of other mammals
and birds who are closer to us in the animal kingdom, but
even of bees. The compound eyes of the *Apis mellifera* can
see things mysterious to us, the unknowable colors in the ultraviolet range, and the degrees of polarized light, which en-

able them to locate the position of the sun even on a cloudy day. Our understanding of our auditory systems had been enhanced by the study of whales and dolphins. As Dr. Schpizhof, my mentor in neuroanatomy, would say, "The more you know, the more you see." This philosophy and practice has refined my thinking and discernment even in the world of manuscripts.

Whenever possible I have met with local private collectors. Many great works of historical, literary, and artistic value are still in the hands of individuals. This may seem unfair, a disservice to the public, but for the most part these manuscripts have been well loved and protected. One can argue that it has been the private solitary individual who was responsible for commissioning these treasures in the first place and for protecting them over the centuries. They must be given their due. They teach us what we must treasure.

Collectors are a diverse lot. Often they are wealthy men and women, but sometimes they are people of more restricted means with one interesting thing, perhaps two or three, that have been in their family or that they have wisely or by fortunate circumstances been able to acquire. Many of these people are naturally cautious about strangers, and such meetings and viewings of their possessions are not easy to accomplish. Proper introductions can be difficult to arrange. Still, if I managed to let it be known that in my youth I had encountered the legendary *Augsburg Miscellany*, otherwise very private and secret doors would open. The *Augsburg Miscellany* had been rarely displayed. Only close friends and respected colleagues of the Laquedem family had been allowed to see it. Once, in 1912, Enoch Laquedem's father, Augustin Laquedem, had allowed it to be displayed publicly at the Jewish Museum in Prague, in a small exhibit held at the Ceremonial Hall of the Burial Society. But this display lasted no more than two days. Augustin Laquedem became so nervous he withdrew the miscellany from view.

"You've seen the *Augsburg Miscellany*?" I am asked in astonishment. "What happened to it?"

"I don't know," I answer.

"But you knew the owner?"

"A long time ago."

"Wasn't he a rabbi from Czechoslovakia? Where did you meet him?"

"Yes, he was from Prague. He was not a rabbi, but he was a great scholar. I never met him. I met his daughter when I was still a boy. She was the owner then."

"His daughter? Where?"

"In Canada. She was visiting for a while. A refugee. She showed it to me. But I've never seen her again. She left quite suddenly. I do not know what happened to her."

"Well, the miscellany seems to have disappeared from the face of the earth. What a great loss! Can you tell us about it? There aren't even any photographs."

I do my best to describe the miscellany to them.

Over time I have come to be a minor expert and connoisseur. I have slowly managed to build up a small collection of my own. Modest in size perhaps, but very fine. I have an illuminated prayer book of the French-Jewish rite from fourteenth-century Troyes, and an illuminated Esther Scroll from the eighteenth-century Austro-Hungarian Empire. In addition, I have three manuscripts of various latter Midrashic commentaries ranging from the twelfth to fifteenth centuries, with various textual variations and emendations. In one of these, a Midrash on the Book of Joshua, I have found a rare allusion to labyrinths in an ancient Hebrew text:

And in the days of Isaac our father, the city of Jericho was built by seven idolatrous kings. And each king built a wall around the city. And any traveler who wished to enter the city of Jericho would circle its walls seven times. But for those who dwelled in the city there were secret doors and they entered at their ease.

And the Garden of Eden likewise has seven walls. And the wicked cannot enter, neither with the sounding of trumpets nor with the circling of its walls, but the righteous shall enter directly through its secret doors.

Recently I acquired a letter from Bellejeune, the daughter of the great eleventh-century scholar Rashi, to her fiancé, Vasselin. She wrote in anticipation of her departure from Troyes to his town of Mayence after the High Holidays:

My beloved. I imagine you nearby watching me, waiting for me as I await your presence.

Bellejeune then quotes a verse from the Song of Songs:

Domeh dodi . . . My beloved is like a gazelle or a
young hart: behold he stands behind our wall, he looks
in at the windows.

In the last decade or so, I have begun to experience a strange phenomenon. Important collectors and museums will seek me out before making certain purchases of their own. Often they have heard of me in a distant way, from someone who knows someone who has met me. It is one of the mysteries of the world and the human race, that we are all somehow connected across oceans and continents and time. There are imperceptible threads and ties that extend on and on from one person to the next, so in the end everyone is bound up in one another.

More recently several institutions and libraries have approached me for different and somewhat alarming reasons.

Usually they begin, "Have you considered, Doctor, where to leave your precious legacy?" or more brazenly, "And how is your health? We heard you have not been so well recently."

"I am quite well," I tell them. "I've never been better."

So far I have avoided making any decision about what I will do with my collection, although the time has already come when I should. I have never been able to think like Eva, that once I have owned something, I will always own it, and so be able to consider relinquishing it as she almost relinquished the *Augsburg Miscellany* that afternoon in the

Statler Hotel. I have not reached this level. Owning, not just preserving, something beautiful *is* important to me. Perhaps it is a form of covetousness and greed, a sin that can lead to others. But I tell myself, although this is only a part truth, that I must think of Asa, and what would happen to him if anything happened to me. After all those years of fragile grace, he is blind.

My own collection, even if modest, is extremely valuable, and continues to increase in value. It has been a guarantee for almost all contingencies. Only now with the recent financial success that has come with my book do I feel more secure. I know that Asa will be well provided for and money is no longer an excuse. But still I am unable to contemplate or plan for when I will be gone from this world.

DURING THE WEEKS that Eva lived with us, she would show us only a page or two of the miscellany at a time, always with great care and as if each time was an important occasion. When she left us she had still not shown us all of its marvels.

Only a few manuscripts in the entire world can compare to the *Augsburg Miscellany*. There is the lavish *Rothschild Miscellany* and the *Farhi Bible*, to name two. Despite its relatively modest size—the size of two hands held open—the *Augsburg Miscellany* was over six hundred pages. Its script was written in black and gold on the finest calf's vellum. As the term implies, the miscellany was composed of diverse works and treatises. In addition to the Book of Psalms, to which Eva had turned that first day she came to Windsor, there were the books of Proverbs, Lamentations, and Esther, the latter with an obscure Midrashic commentary that Enoch Laquedem had translated and published at his expense. The volume contained weekday, Sabbath, and holiday prayers, a Passover Haggadah of the Italian rite, as well as philosophical, astronomical, and moral treatises. There was a bestiary depicting the animals of the world and their spiritual and medicinal attributes, and even a small treatise on music, both rare subjects in Hebrew manuscripts.

The *Augsburg Miscellany* was lavishly decorated with full-page miniatures, as well as numerous initial-word panels, and marginal illustrations including a depiction of the Pillar of Cloud that led the Children of Israel through the wilderness for forty years and which so inspired Enoch Laquedem as a child.

AFTER THE NAZIS entered Czechoslovakia and began abolishing the Jewish communities of Bohemia and Moravia, a strange series of tedious and dangerous negotiations began between representatives of the besieged Prague Jewish community and the Nazi-run Zentralamt für die Regelung der Judenfrage—the Central Office for Regulation of the Jewish Question.

In an attempt to preserve whatever they might of their threatened culture, the representatives of the dwindling community sought to convince the invaders to preserve the Jewish Museum of Prague. According to the archival record, which I saw decades later in Prague, these representatives included Professor Dr. Enoch Laquedem. Among the Nazi officials with whom the delegation met was Adolf Eichmann, who was later brought to trial in Jerusalem.

The destroyers finally agreed to a plan to maintain the Jewish Museum. For their own propaganda purposes, they reinstituted the museum under their control. In the few documents that remain, they referred to it as the Museum for an Extinct Race. Perhaps, they also thought, by maintaining the museum, they might more easily acquire the treasures of the communities throughout Bohemia and Moravia that they ordered dismantled.

I cannot help thinking that in a bizarre way they had anticipated a future and overpowering nostalgia for the people they had undertaken to destroy. And so they needed memento mori.

For the activities of the "newly reorganized" museum the Nazis conscripted experts from the other Jewish museums that had been established in prewar Czechoslovakia and forced to close. These scholars included Dr. Josef Polák, director of the museum in Košice; Professor Dr. Alfred Engel, founder of the museum in Mikulov; and Dr. Salomon Hugo Lieben, one of the original founders of the Prague Museum at the turn of the century.

The doomed staff worked endless hours sorting and cataloguing the hundreds of thousands of goods—among them rare books, ritual objects, synagogue ornaments—that were confiscated from communities and private owners throughout Czechoslovakia and sent to Prague.

Perhaps in the most perverse twist to life in the museum, the doomed scholars were directed to create various exhibits for visiting Nazi officials of the highest rank. As if one were forced to prepare one's own brain for dissection.

In the archives of the Jewish Museum, I found the catalogue for a large display of Hebrew manuscripts and printing that was held in the sixteenth-century High Synagogue on Cervená Street. The entries were written by the librarian Professor Dr. Tobiáš Jakobovits and Enoch Laquedem. That they were credited for their scholarly work, as if in normal times, was yet another touch of Nazi perversity.

In the catalogue entry for the *De Braga Maḥzor*, a prayer book that had been owned by a Jewish family in Brno and brought to Prague during the confiscations, Laquedem wrote:

> *This elaborately illustrated prayer book was commissioned by the court Jew Solomon De Braga for personal use and completed in 1437 in southern Germany. The illuminator and scribe, Alexander of Augsburg, had mastered the most sophisticated techniques used by the great artists of his day both in Italy and in France. He went on to innovate and acquire his own unique style in which scenes of sky, water, or atmospheric phenomena are made translucent, showing within them the power and various manifestations of the Creator. Alexander of Augsburg, believed by many to be the most gifted illuminator of his time, was responsible for several Hebrew*

masterpieces, including the legendary Augsburg Miscellany, which has been lost in modern times.

When I read this I was astonished. No doubt it was extremely dangerous for Enoch Laquedem to mention the *Augsburg Miscellany* in the catalogue. What if someone inquired into its provenance and whereabouts? Perhaps he could not control himself. Perhaps he thought it important and worth the risk to somehow, even in a catalogue written for the destroyers, preserve the knowledge that a work such as the *Augsburg Miscellany* had indeed existed even while his daughter secretly smuggled it to relative safety without his initial knowledge and against his wishes. Perhaps he desperately wanted to believe in a future time when the destroyers would be defeated, and the miscellany and his daughter returned to him.

CHAPTER 14

HE MORNING AFTER SHE AR-
rived at our house, Eva stayed in her room
and did not come down for breakfast.

My mother said, "Eva must be exhausted. So much happened to her yesterday."

By mid-morning my mother became
concerned. "I hope Eva's feeling well," she
said to me. "So much happened to her yesterday, it must be so upsetting."

This made me very worried, too.

I followed my mother upstairs. She
tapped lightly on Eva's door. "Eva, would
you like something to eat? I can still make
you some breakfast."

My mother put her ear to the door and knocked some-what harder. "Eva, are you feeling all right?"

Finally Eva answered softly through the door. "Yes, I'm fine, Adele. Just a moment."

Asa came rushing up the stairs. He was all out of breath and shaking. "What happened? Is Eva dead?"

"God forbid, Asa!" my mother said.

"Well, every single one of our boarders died in that room, except mean Iris May! But she was only here a few days. She would have died, too, if she had stayed any longer. There's a curse on this house! We should move."

My mother spoke calmly. "Really, Asa, that's nonsense. Control yourself. We've only had one boarder who died, Mr. Applewine, and he was old and unwell. It's natural for old people to die. We've talked about that many times. And it's not nice to talk of Iris May like that. Iris May was very nice to you. She gave you a nice book."

Asa began chanting, "Nice, nice, nice, nice, nice, nice."

We heard Eva's voice behind the door. "I'm fine."

"Then what are you doing?" Asa asked.

She opened the door wide and stood back a foot or two inside the room. She was wearing a full-length violet dress-ing gown. A tall, elongated whooping crane in silver embroi-dery stretched up all along its side. Her luxurious hair was done up as elegantly and perfectly as it had been the day be-fore, held up by the two silver bird-head pins.

"Oh, Eva," my mother said. "I'm . . . I'm sorry we dis-turbed you. I was worried—"

"Please come in."

We all hesitated at the doorway. She beckoned us forward with her hand.

Overnight the drab sunroom was transformed. An orange-and-gold brocade cloth was spread over the bed, and a smaller piece of matching fabric was draped over the back of the love seat. On the walls, in place of the faded pictures of Lake Huron, hung two long calligraphy scrolls in Chinese characters and a woodblock print of Mount Fuji. The door of one closet was ajar and I caught a glimpse of several brilliant colors. I had the embarrassing and covetous notion that I would like to have these exotic things for myself. It suddenly occurred to me that even if I was not beautiful, at least I could have beautiful things. And if I had beautiful things like Eva had, I would be much happier.

Eva smiled. "I feel right at home, now, with all my ornaments, despite my little speech yesterday. Though I meant every word I said." She swept one hand through the air. "I really could live without all these possessions. They are not much really. Just a few things to cheer me up."

She crouched as she had the previous day and put her face level to Asa's.

"Now, Asa, do I look like I am dying?"

"No."

"Oh, Eva," my mother said. "It looks so lovely in here."

"It's nothing, really. Just an illusion. Why don't we have a little visit, and then I need to do my work. I have so much to do. I have neglected my duties for so long. It's as if I have been in a trance for years. Like in some fairy tale, where the girl is turned into a statue or a swan.

"Please, everyone sit down."

Asa and I sat on the love seat. My mother sat on a chair.

"What's this?" Asa said, picking up a small golden figurine from the night table.

"That is the magical giraffe who was brought to the emperor's zoo. Have I told you yet about the emperor's zoo?"

"We just met you yesterday," Asa said.

"Yes, that's true. Well then, I will tell you now. Long, long ago the Mongolians conquered China. The Great Emperor of Mongolia moved his capital to what is now Beijing.

"Are you listening closely? There are many details."

We nodded.

Eva told us how the Great Emperor of Mongolia had created a zoo with the most amazing creatures in the world. There was Abulabaz, the elephant who was raised in the Himalayas by nightingales. When he was brought to the capital, Abulabaz studied opera with the greatest performers of the time. His tenor voice could make your heart melt. He possessed such great stage presence that he was always given starring roles.

"Though of course he was very fussy about his roles and could be quite difficult. Still, all the lady stars wanted to appear with him. One even left her husband and children to marry him!"

Then there were the two enormous freshwater fish, Eldad and Medad, big as whales. They lived in an artificial lake within the palace grounds. At night, Eldad and Medad would climb out of their lake and play on land, hiding in the darkness.

"Eldad and Medad are no doubt relatives of the Leviathan," Eva explained. "They were not as large, of course. The real Leviathan, if it moved on land, would cause earthquakes." She was thoughtful for a moment. "As a matter of fact, that may be the source of some earthquakes.

"And of course in the garden were Solomon's bees, which live forever.

"Anyway, the emperor's rarest and most precious acquisition, the unicorn, which the Chinese call the qilin, never even made it to the zoo, though the emperor did not ever realize this. The emperor sold a third of his kingdom to purchase the qilin just to please his favorite wife."

"What was his favorite wife's name?" Asa asked.

Eva made a loud shrieking sound that came from high up in her nasal cavities.

We jumped in our seats.

"Sorry, but that's her name. You asked and so there was no way to avoid it. But I will repeat it softer this time."

Even the second time we could not really hear the name properly. It sounded to my ears like, *L'ou'a L'ou'a*.

"L'ou'a L'ou'a was very spoiled and babyish and nagging." Eva imitated her in a squeaky, whining voice. " 'I want a magic qilin for my birthday, otherwise I shall hold my breath and die!' " Eva pinched her nose between her fingers as if she were going to suffocate herself. " 'I want a qilin now!'

"L'ou'a L'ou'a was so spoiled she did not even say, 'Please!'

"The emperor was so crazy in love with L'ou'a L'ou'a that in a great rush to satisfy her he sent off an expedition to Madagascar, which has all the most wonderful creatures that God called forth at the beginning of the world.

"But the leader of the expedition made a grave mistake. He was in a hurry to get back to China before the storm season began.

"They should have waited until they found the qilin's mate, and brought them together. A foolish miscalculation. More foolish than my silly misunderstanding about my visa! Everyone knows that unicorns are very sensitive and have the most fragile hearts. The poor unicorn died at sea."

Asa watched Eva wide-eyed.

"Well, Admiral Zheng He, the leader of the expedition, did not know what to do. The emperor would have been very angry not to have his unicorn. So they stopped on the coast of Africa and brought back a giraffe, which the emperor and his court had never seen. Have you ever seen a giraffe, Asa?"

"Of course. They have them in the Detroit Zoo."

"I see. Yes. I should have realized that. In America there are many wonders. And every one is welcome and at home, including the giraffes, who don't even need visas! Well, this was no simple zoo giraffe but a magical one that could read minds and cast spells."

Eva went over to the bed and pulled her orange-and-gold cloth from the bed in one swift motion. In a moment she whirled around and draped herself with it so she was a shimmering orange-and-gold creature.

"Voilà! The magical giraffe!"

Eva trotted around the room with two fingers held over her abundant red hair. Her feet were turned out ever so slightly like little hooves.

It was a delightful scene. I had goose bumps all over my body. I had never had such a strange and wonderful feeling.

My mother and Asa giggled, clapping their hands.

"Fortunately, the emperor had never seen a giraffe before and he was fooled. He thought it was indeed the sacred qilin. A great celebration was held with days and days of banquets for all the empire's great personages and the ambassadors from far away, from Portugal and the Empire of the Ottomans, also from Timbuktu and Holland.

"The court poet composed a poem of praise."

Eva, still draped in the bedspread, recited the long poem of praise in a singsong:

> O *Auspicious visitor,*
> O *noble creature, our celestial qilin,*
> *we see your gentle glory*
> *our joy knows no end*
> *you do not eat flesh*
> *your hooves do not tread on living things*
> *and when you wander*
> *Fortune guides your way!*
> *You send your wisdom before you!*
> *The mother of Confucius*
> *was blessed by you!*

"It was a moment of high poetic achievement but one of the emperor's other wives was very jealous of L'ou'a L'ou'a and wanted to make trouble. She blurted out, '*That* is not the sacred qilin! It is only a deformed horse!'

"The music in the great hall stopped. All heads turned. The giraffe regarded the wife with one of her eyes." Eva turned the side of her face to us and looked at us out of the corner of one large green eye. Eva blinked several times. For a moment she reminded me of Nebuchadnezzar when he turned his head to look at something.

"The giraffe spoke in Hebrew and Chinese! '*Lev rah! Lashon ra'ah!*'—'Oh, wicked heart! Oh, Evil tongue!'

"A shudder swept through the banquet hall. The noble creature had spoken! Indeed the people believed more than ever that this must be the sacred qilin."

"What happened!"

"The woman could not speak. Her voice disappeared. Forever! She was instantly banished from the empire for disturbing the sacred qilin. She spent the rest of her days wandering the world."

"But she was telling the truth, Eva!" Asa said. "You're not supposed to lie. It wasn't a qilin. You said so!"

Eva stood there a moment carefully considering Asa's question. She let the bedspread slip from around her and fall to the floor. She stepped forward. She was no longer a magical giraffe but a tall and elegant woman in a violet dressing gown with a whooping crane on the side.

She spoke very softly, almost in a whisper.

"Yes, Asa, one should always tell the truth; there is nothing more important than the truth. Your mother would be very upset with me if I told you otherwise." She nodded at my mother. "But there are times, extreme situations, when one should not speak. The other wife should have kept silent. She was only trying to harm another living being. Do you know what terrible things could have happened to the giraffe? It was not her fault they mistook her for something she was not, was it? Everyone was happy with her. She was a good-natured creature. And what really was there to be gained?" Eva paused a moment and then said, her voice wavering ever so slightly, "Do you think I was wrong to lie about the little girl who traveled with me on the train through Siberia? Do you think I am a liar because I said the little girl was my daughter and helped her escape from the terrible war and the people who would have killed her?"

"No," Asa said.

"What ever happened to the little girl, Eva?" my mother asked.

"She went on to Shanghai and was taken in by relatives who had already gone there. I have tried to find out what happened but have not heard anything from her since. Her grandfather was a friend of my father's."

"Oh, my," my mother said.

Eva smiled again. "Well, that is the end of the story. And now I hope you will excuse me." She nodded toward the desk on which she had placed a handwritten manuscript and another ream of paper. "I have so much to do. I don't know where to start! I need to finish my father's book. I promised I would. It is written in his difficult handwriting and some chapters are incomplete. I have put off so many things. I had to take care of my dear husband. He was sick for several years."

"Is there anything we can do to help you, Eva?" my mother said.

"May I use your husband's typewriter?"

"Yes, of course," my mother said. "I'll go get it for you. Would you like some breakfast, Eva?"

"No, thank you. It is a great responsibility to finish my father's book. Right now I do not even care about food or water. They are not important."

"You have to eat something."

"Perhaps a cup of coffee would be welcome. And something light, not too much trouble, maybe two poached eggs. Would you mind?"

"My pleasure. Would you like toast?"

"Oh, no thank you. I had toast last night. Do you have any more cheese?"

"Of course, Eva."

"Do you have a different kind?"

"Last night I served you cheddar, but I also have American."

Eva considered a moment. "Yes, I'd like to try that."

My mother ushered us out of Eva's room. "We must do everything to help Eva get along with her work. It is terribly important. The poor thing. I'm sure it is very hard to finish her father's book. But she is so learned. If anyone is up to the task, she is."

CHAPTER 15

A WHILE LATER I KNOCKED ON the door to bring Eva the coffee, poached eggs, and American cheese my mother had prepared for her.

Eva opened the door just wide enough for me to see her face. "Thank you so much, Joseph. This looks delicious. Is this milk? I hate to trouble anyone again. Does your mother have any cream?"

I went down and brought back a small pitcher of cream.

"Thank you, Joseph. You are all so kind to me. I'll bring the tray down later. Are you practicing your reading this morning?"

"Yes. It's a lot of work."

"Yes, it is. I'm looking forward to hearing you read. I know you will do an excellent job. You are very studious and intelligent, Joseph, just like my father was when he was your age. I have to admit, it is not easy for me to concentrate and study. I always have to force myself."

She then made a small wave with her hand, smiled at me, and closed her door.

Eva's withdrawal into her room that first morning affected all of us. I had trouble concentrating on practicing the *parsha*. I kept thinking of Eva trotting around the sunroom like a magical giraffe. I tried to remember every movement she had made and picture it over and over in my mind so I would never forget. I kept hearing her say, "You are very studious and intelligent, Joseph, just like my father was when he was your age."

Meanwhile Asa was running around the house opening and closing venetian blinds and curtains. For the first time that I could remember, my mother burned one of her cakes. "I don't know what's gotten into Asa this morning," she said. "He's driving me crazy!"

A few hours later, Eva came out of her room. She called from the top of the stairs.

"Hello! Hello! Where is everybody?"

We gathered at the foot of the stairs.

"Oh, I thought you may have all gone out. I'm so glad you're all still here."

She looked down and smiled at us. She wore a lilac-colored satin dress with black high heels.

My mother held her hands to her chest. "Eva. You look like a movie star!"

"Thank you, Adele. Oh dear, I forgot the breakfast tray!"
Eva looked around her as if she could not figure out what to
do next, or how to get out of the predicament of having forgotten the breakfast tray. It did not occur to any of us that
this apparent confusion was odd considering her no doubt
more difficult and complex travels across the world even in
times of war.

"Don't worry about the tray. I'll get it later," my mother said.

Eva looked relieved. "Thank you, Adele. Once I'm really
settled in I will be more helpful. Sometimes I feel totally
lost!"

"That's understandable, Eva. You've been through so
much. I hope you were able to get some work done this
morning on your father's book."

"No. I did not have time. I had to compose several important messages. I was hoping there was a telegraph office
nearby so I could send them. I need to find some old friends
and acquaintances of my father. But I do not know who has
survived or where they have gone. My father came to me in
a dream and told me I was too cut off from the world I came
from. I know it is only a dream but I feel I should do something about it."

"Yes, Eva, you should," my mother said, "but you can
arrange a telegram over the phone."

"I'd rather walk and do it in person. It's such a lovely day.
I always like to get to know the place I'm living in." She then
quoted Moses, who commanded the twelve spies that he

sent into Canaan, " *'U're'isem* . . . And you shall see the land, what it is, and the people that dwelleth therein!' "

"Eva, I can't get over how well you know the *chumash*," my mother said.

My mother hesitated a moment. "I know you have so much work to do, Eva, but would you teach me about the hapax legomena? I've been thinking about them all last night and this morning."

"Yes, of course." Eva smiled. "We will do that this evening. And perhaps you will all help me learn about this wonderful country. I would also like to open an account at the bank. Which bank do you use?"

"The Imperial Bank of Commerce."

"Imperial? Sounds very secure. Is it?"

"Yes, of course, Eva. This is Canada."

"I suppose they have international connections. I will need them to contact my bank in Switzerland. Is it the best bank?"

"It's an excellent bank but there are several others, too. My husband used to keep an account at the Bank of Montreal. But it's too late to go to the bank today. It's almost three o'clock already."

"Then I will just go to the telegraph office."

Asa said, "Can I go with you, Eva?"

"Yes, of course. I was just going to ask your mother if you could take me. We can try out the silk." She then looked at my mother. "Adele, may Asa take me?"

"It would be wonderful if you went with Asa. He needs

to get out of the house more. He only goes out when it's raining."

"Do you know the way to the telegraph office, Asa?"

"Of course I do."

"Yes, I knew you would."

Eva stood on the landing. She was searching for something in her handbag. I was jealous that Asa was going with her. Why did she ask Asa to go with her and not me? Didn't she say I reminded her of her father? Why didn't she want me to come with her? But Eva then said, "Would you join us, too, Joseph?"

Part of me wanted to say no, I cannot go, I am too busy, you should have asked me first. But then the rest of me wanted so badly to join them. I realized I was sometimes ill-tempered, saying I did not want to do something when I really did want to do it.

"Yes, I'll go," I said, although aside from my cranky character I knew I should be practicing the *parsha*. I had already worked very hard on it that week, but I felt insecure, especially as I had wasted so much time that morning day-dreaming. I would have to work harder that evening.

We followed Eva out the front door. Asa put on his sunglasses and the silk veiling. Eva wrapped a piece of sheer turquoise silk over her hair.

"There's a touch of a breeze today," she said.

Asa ran down the porch stairs and looked up at the sky.

"Asa, please be careful," Eva said. "You still mustn't look directly at the sun. But you can look everywhere else in the sky, which is very large, don't you think?"

Out on the porch Eva stood near the trellis and gently drew one of the roses to her nose. She inhaled deeply.

I had the alarming notion that all the roses were terribly afraid. I thought I could feel their fear transmitted to me. It had never occurred to me before that flowers could have feelings and I was confused by this perception. It made me feel nauseated.

Eva said, "Oh, no, no, I didn't mean to upset you."

At first I thought she was speaking to me and then I realized she was talking to the flower. "I will not pick you," she said and released her frail captive. It retreated back among the other flowers.

Eva turned to me. "One mustn't return kindness with cruelty. The roses were very kind to me yesterday. I think they learned their kindness from you. I can tell you appreciate beautiful things, Joseph. That's why you take such care of the roses." She touched me gently on my shoulder. "My father always told me that plants and flowers have souls. How else could wise King Solomon have spoken to them? He wouldn't have had much conversation with them if they hadn't had souls! We have to respect all growing things even if we do not understand their ways."

She then walked down the stairs, looking this way then that.

Her words were a revelation. Now I understood why I was so drawn to the roses. Not just because they were the most exquisite and fragrant of flowers, but because they each had a little soul.

Eva said, "Where are you running to, Asa? Come take my

hand. You know, boys, there are so many pretty trees here! It's one of the first things I noticed when I arrived. Where I lived in Japan we mostly had pine trees, not oaks and elms, though we had the loveliest trees in Prague.

"Why don't we walk in the shade?"

WE WALKED UP Victoria Avenue toward downtown and the river.

We must have made a striking procession, Asa with gossamer blue fluttering around his head holding hands with Eva in a lilac-colored satin dress and turquoise silk around her splendid hair.

Though I was happy to be with Eva, I felt apart from them. They seemed so perfect together and I did not truly belong to the picture they made. Asa laughed and pointed to things. Eva, towering above him, inclined her head just so and asked him a question. Although it was strange to see Asa wearing the silk scarf over his head, I thought that people would understand and accept what they saw without criticism. They would understand, not because it was explained to them that Asa's retinas were degenerating, and he believed the sun was destroying them and that the silk would protect him, but because Eva and Asa were so beautiful and nothing else mattered.

ON OUELLETTE AVENUE, we walked several blocks until we reached the telegraph office. Along the way people would stop to look at Eva, more so than they used to look at Asa. Eva did not seem to notice this attention at all, just as Asa never seemed to notice the attention he received. She simply looked straight ahead or at the different trees and buildings.

The telegraph office was dark and smoky. Eva stood in line for the clerk.

Isabel Kremlach came into the lobby. She carried a gift box tied with string.

"Why, Joseph and Asa, I thought I saw you through the window. What are you wearing, Asa?"

"It's silk to protect my eyes from the sun."

"Silk? Where did you get such a fine piece of material? Do you know how expensive it is? I never saw that color on your mother, though I keep telling her she should wear more color. She doesn't have to look like Nebuchadnezzar, but a little red or purple would be cheerful, don't you think?"

"Our new boarder gave it to me. She's from Japan."

"Did you say Japan? You have a new boarder?"

Asa turned and pointed to Eva in line.

"*¡Dios mío!* She is something. But she doesn't look Japanese to me, Asa. Are you sure she is from Japan?" She switched to a quiet voice. "She's very tall. Taller than your mother and Joseph."

"She's a scientist. Her husband was a doctor. She lived in Japan for ten years."

Isabel said, "Oh, I see. Why don't you boys introduce us? I love meeting new people."

Asa took Isabel over to Eva in line.

Eva smiled. "I am Eva Higashi."

"So nice to meet you," Isabel said. "I hear you are a scientist. What kind?"

"I am a biologist. But my studies were interrupted by the war."

"Oh, that's too bad," Isabel said. "But at least you got away. *El que no tiene cabeza ha de tener pies*—whoever doesn't have a head should have feet!" Isabel held up her package. "My niece in Havana is a nurse and just had a little girl. I bought her an adorable two-piece outfit at Smith's. It's a very fine store if you want to know. My niece is only married a year. I'm so glad she didn't have the troubles having a baby that I had. Sometimes these things run in families and then of course the family dies out. I was just passing by when I saw Adele's boys."

"Congratulations on the baby," Eva said.

"Thank you. It's very nice to have a new face in town. I'm so glad Adele has a woman boarder. That poor old Mr. Applewine was so depressing. My husband gave the eulogy but there really wasn't much to say, God forgive my tongue. I remember because my husband had a terrible cold and the weather was awful but still he had to do his duty. A rabbi is just like a doctor only he isn't paid as well. It's much better for Adele to have a young woman around. I'm sure the boys would agree!"

"Iris May stayed with us for three days and she was more creepy than Mr. Applewine," Asa said. "She never looks at you when she talks."

Mrs. Kremlach smiled and patted Asa on the head. "It's just Iris May's artistic temperament, Asa. Artists are shy creatures. But we do need them, as much as we need rabbis and scientists. Otherwise the world becomes very dull and nothing changes."

Suddenly she said to me very sweetly, "Are you all prepared for this Shabbes? You know you are a lifesaver, Joseph *muñeco*. Otherwise with Zubrovsky gone my poor husband would have to prepare everything, and you know how overworked he is already. Do you know how many people are in Hôtel Dieu this week? Six! And he has to visit them all again before Shabbes. You're lucky to have such a learned mother who can teach you properly." She whispered, "I think you will even do a better job than my husband."

She turned to Eva. "Did you know that Joseph and our Adele were so learned?"

"Yes."

"Next!" the telegraph clerk announced.

"Please excuse me." Eva moved to the counter.

At the counter I heard Eva saying, "Of course, I shall have to spell them out for you. They are not in English."

Isabel said to me, "Joseph, why don't you bring your friend when you come to visit Nebuchadnezzar? Nebuchadnezzar loves meeting new people, especially charming scientists."

CHAPTER 16

I N THE LATE 1950S, WHILE STILL in medical school, I chose to pursue a research career. I had realized that clinical medicine and the life of a practitioner would not, after all, suit me. Perhaps this reflects poorly on my character, which I've always known has been flawed and limited. Although I enjoyed the science, the anatomy, physiology, and pharmacology that I studied, I knew I would not be adept at what is called the art of medicine, the intuitive insight, the compassionate distance, and the open engagement with living things.

During medical school, I began working during the little spare time I had in the laboratory of Dr. Zachary Schpizhof, renowned for his work in human and comparative neuroanatomy.

Dr. Schpizhof had built his reputation on researching those structures with which we humans and many other creatures experience sight, the optic lobes and visual cortex. Schpizhof had done elegant and celebrated work in birds and mammals, including man. He also taught a course in human neuroanatomy to the medical students. To the students he was known for the thought-provoking things he said.

"When we study neuroanatomy we must not fool ourselves into thinking we are studying 'life' or the 'soul.' The specimen is only a shadow, there is no 'life' or 'soul' there anymore," or "Anatomy is after all a visual discipline, and limited by our visual abilities. There are dimensions to our being that we will never understand or imagine because they require senses we do not possess."

When I began working in his laboratory, Schpizhof was already a bit weary, near the end of his career. He was contemplating a future on the Costa Blanca, where he had bought a small house. In his conversations he liked to sprinkle the Spanish words he was learning as a preparation for his new life. On one of the laboratory walls, above the long file cabinet in which he kept reprints of his numerous articles, was a photograph of a small white villa with an orange tile roof and surrounded by bougainvillea. In the distance was the sea.

"In my new career I will concentrate on plant life, *el reino vegetal,* Joseph. I will tend grapevines and oranges. I will have nothing more to do with vertebrates! Except, of course, my dear wife."

One evening soon after I began working in his laboratory, he invited me to his house for dinner. His wife, Shinobu, smiled as he escorted me into his library. There he opened a glass book cabinet. Out of it he took a rare original edition of the classic text written by the Spanish neuroanatomist Santiago Ramón y Cajal, *Textura del sistema nervioso del hombre y de los vertebrados—Texture of the Nervous System of Man and of the Vertebrates.*

Schpizhof slowly opened the *Textura,* so beautifully illustrated in Cajal's own hand. Although many of the illustrations in that old book were faded, I felt deeply moved, as I had that afternoon years before when Eva came to live with us and first showed us the *Augsburg Miscellany.* I was most fascinated by Cajal's exquisite drawing of a Purkinje cell, the most elaborate nerve cell in the brain. With its innumerable branching dendrites, this neuron resembles an old and venerable windswept tree.

Sitting in Schpizhof's library, looking into the *Textura,* I felt I was seeing the various microscopic structures of the nervous system as Cajal had encountered them, as a revelation, as if I were seeing not only them, but myself for the first time.

I had the startling image of the great Cajal peering into a microscope, a brain longingly seeking its own self, or perhaps love, in the brains of so many other diverse creatures. It occurred to me then, as it often has since when I find an exceptional manuscript, that the power of the drawings comes directly from the life of the artist. In the case of the *Textura*, I felt this power was coming from the late Dr. Cajal.

When I entered Schpizhof's laboratory, I had no idea what research I might undertake. For a short while I helped him on a project he was finishing on the optic lobes of the sparrow. A few simple drawings from an earlier phase of that project were displayed in the hallway outside his laboratory, in a floor-to-ceiling glass case called "The Gallery of Anatomy."

After a month or so Schpizhof suggested I work on an aspect of the limbic system of man. Perhaps I could help him answer an anatomical question that had been a subject of intense speculation in the scientific world, and whose answer might shed light on whether a certain structure on the inner aspect of the temporal lobe was the seat of memory or emotion.

About this time my mother died from a chronic and debilitating disease. I had come back to Windsor as often as I could during her illness, and then for her funeral. Although Asa's vision had already declined in recent years, he had finished his undergraduate degree at Assumption College and taken constant and loving care of my mother. He never complained of this hardship. I do not believe he found it so. He never once asked for my help. He seemed content with the busy if quiet life he had at home. But now that my mother was gone he did not want to be alone.

Asa was even more beautiful in those days than he was as a child. He had become an exquisite young man, perfectly proportioned, finely featured. He was oblivious to it all as he had been during his childhood. Only a slight stoop to his shoulders marred his appearance.

Many people visited our house that week of shiva out of respect and affection for my mother. Rabbi and Isabel Kremlach came. Rabbi Kremlach repeated what he had said of her at the eulogy, that my mother was an uncommonly wise and learned woman. He said to us, "I'm still amazed and inspired that she went back to school and got her master's degree."

Isabel apologized for Ruchi's absence, he was still away, but doing "much better these days." She could barely hold back her tears when she told me how their beloved Nebuchadnezzar had recently died. "He really was a genius," Isabel said. "*El gran genio.*" She changed the subject and forced herself to smile. "We are all so proud of you, Joseph *muñeco.*"

I was particularly touched when Mr. Zubrovsky and Iris May came to our house with their daughter to pay their condolences. Miriam was almost ten. Although I had been to Windsor many times in the previous years, I had not run into Iris May.

Iris May had changed since she had married. I did not recognize her at first.

"You know, Joseph," she said, laughing, "your mother was the most honest woman I knew, but she did tell a lie once. She said I would never be fat."

One afternoon during that week of shiva, Asa and I found ourselves alone. It was fall but the day had turned unseasonably warm. We went into the backyard. Everywhere the flowerbeds were overgrown and covered with leaves. I was suddenly very sad. Now that my mother was gone, the house and the yard seemed lifeless, too.

I told Asa how grateful I was he had taken such loving care of our mother.

"I should have been more helpful, Asa. I should have come home more often. I knew Mother was dying."

I started crying.

Asa touched me gently on the arm. "I am very proud of what you are doing, Joseph. Mother was, too." He then quoted softly, " 'The Day of Death is hidden, but the Holy One Blessed be He and His ministering angels hold the days of our lives in their hands.' "

For a moment Asa became very quiet. He then asked me what I was doing in the laboratory.

I explained to Asa the project I was working on with Schpizhof. I mentioned the difficulties in drawing the complex neural pathways connecting different parts of the brain.

I was thinking out loud, really. It made me feel better to talk of these things. Perhaps I was going on a bit too long.

Asa suddenly said, "Maybe I could help with your work, Joseph."

Though I knew he had always drawn very well, I was skeptical that he could be of use, especially with his visual limitations. I did not know what to say. I did not want to hurt his feelings, especially at such a time. Somehow I felt the loss of our mother was an even greater blow to him.

I caught the old pleading look in his face.

"I'm sure I could help you, Joseph. You need me, I can

tell. You're not taking care of yourself either." He touched me again on the arm. "You look tired and skinny, Joseph. Let me at least try."

I could not bear to turn him down. As it turned out, ours became a collaboration that was to last most of my academic life and was invaluable to my successful career.

As a teenager, Asa began to lose the peripheral portions of his vision. Luckily, throughout his entire adult life, his vision stabilized and he maintained a useful central field of vision, though he would see the world as if through a tunnel. With care and concentration he has been able to look through this tunnel and understand more than most. Together with Dr. Schpizhof, I was able to modify a magnifying and illuminating device, a camera lucida, which made it easier for Asa to study the dissections I performed and to draw what he saw. Schpizhof even arranged for a small stipend for my brother.

Almost an entire year of intense work, which I did simultaneously with my medical school courses, resulted in my first major paper on the hippocampus, an ancient structure of the brain that is found in various levels of development in all creatures with bony skeletons. "Projections of the Human Hippocampus to the Thalamic Nuclei" appeared in the *Journal of Brain Research*. Schpizhof generously allowed me to be first author while he was second.

Because of the exquisite drawings Asa contributed, Schpizhof agreed to make him third author. Hand in hand with the tedious laboratory work are the meticulous renderings of the findings in drawings. These renderings convey more information than is possible with descriptive words alone.

I was delighted to see my name, even if accompanied by others, in such a distinguished journal. I was amazed to think that my discoveries and ideas, written down and in print, would become part of the collective memory of mankind that resides in all the great scientific and medical libraries of the world. I liked to imagine that long after I was gone, someone, even if only one person, might still stumble upon something I had once written, and for a moment might wonder to themselves, Who was this person? What was he like? How did he come to do what he did?

"Projections of the Human Hippocampus to the Thalamic Nuclei" made a small sensation in the scientific community. Although I still had another year of medical school, I was immediately offered several research positions from various academic institutions. I was told I could do whatever neuroanatomic work I might desire. Instead I chose to remain in Dr. Schpizhof's laboratory. Eventually, after his retirement, he saw to it that it became mine.

N E U R O A N A T O M Y is a meticulous field, painstaking and repetitive. It is at times a primitive if elegant endeavor. All one's efforts are focused on unveiling and describing what is already there, in front of our eyes, merely hidden from our immediate understanding by its infinite complexity.

All anatomy is ancient, reaching back to an unimaginable antiquity, measured in hundreds of thousands and millions of years.

The pleasure for the research anatomist is in the discovery of the structure of life and the design of the spirit that comes down to us through the aeons, born again and again in our world in a myriad of newly breathing creatures. There is a further inexplicable delight in the rendering and illumination of what is found. The paradox remains, as Schpizhof often pointed out, that the very object studied can be approached only through a medium like itself, another human mind, and with that mind's visual sense.

In anatomy, there is no equation or theorem that comes to one in a dream or in a waking revelation. At least that has never happened to me. Sometimes though, while working in the laboratory, one's eyes are suddenly opened like those of the heavenly hosts. In that glorious moment one sees far beyond anything ever seen before by humans, back into the far reaches of time.

By nature I am well suited to the labored and obsessive inquiry that this anatomic research requires. It is advantageous when a lifelong character flaw can be channeled into a formidable strength. That my work has become the main focus of my life may seem limiting to some, but I do not see it that way. I feel I am among the most fortunate of men, that through my work I have experienced so much of the world and, more important, contributed to its understanding.

There are many ways to explore a brain, on gross and microscopic levels, and every year newer ways are developed using the latest advances in biochemistry.

In my research I am now considered a bit old-fashioned. Throughout my career I have continued to use, though not exclusively, what some perceive as an antiquated and quaint technique, a reliable if extremely time-consuming method of nerve fiber dissection. This technique involves an elaborate freezing and thawing process Schpizhof taught me, and that he himself had learned in Switzerland.

Freshly harvested brains of whatever species are bathed and fixed in formaldehyde and then frozen for eight to ten days. They are then set out to thaw. This freezing and thawing process results in the loosening up of the otherwise densely woven structure of the brain. The dissections are then carried out with fine watchmaker forceps with tips made of first-class steel. For even finer dissections, these watchmaker forceps may be too coarse and one must peel the more delicate neural fibers with the tips of snipe feathers, an elegant trick much favored by Schpizhof.

When I first began putting endless hours in his laboratory, Schpizhof said to me, "Ach, Joseph. You are just like your biblical namesake, working seventy years for his wife's hand in marriage!"

I corrected him. "You mean Jacob, the son of Isaac, who worked *seven* years for Leah and another seven years for Rachel and another seven for a share in his father-in-law Laban's livestock."

"Yes, yes. Jacob, son of Isaac. That's who I meant! I was not well educated in these things. I was raised an atheist!

"You are always so precise, Joseph. Nothing slips by you. That is why you will be a great anatomist. But it is good to have imagination, too. Like Asa. That is why his drawings are so extraordinary."

I admit I found myself upset by this comment. It rankled. Did Asa have more imagination than I? He was only drawing what was there, what I revealed to him. But I did not say anything. I was also glad that Schpizhof thought so well of Asa. It would make my life easier. I would be able to watch out for Asa. I felt it was my duty. I knew it would please my mother to know that Asa and I were together, that I was sharing with him all the wonderful things I was learning, and including him in my work.

I often asked Asa if he wanted to go on and get an advanced degree of his own. I realized now there was no reason why he couldn't.

"No, I'm not interested in that. I just don't have your ambitions, Joseph, I'm not sorry to say. I'm content to live as I am. I have everything I need. I have our work together and my friends. I'm never anxious or disappointed like you."

CHAPTER 17

HAT EVENING, THE DAY EVA went for the first time to the telegraph office, she kept her promise to my mother.

The two women sat in the garden chairs around the sundial. It was still light.

I intended to stay only a short while, since I had so much left to do. I had already taken off too much time that afternoon accompanying Eva downtown.

"It is paradise out here!" Eva said, stretching out her long legs. She turned them slightly this way and that, briefly inspecting them. She gently caressed one of her calves.

Then, as if she were casually gossiping with a neighbor, she began explaining to my mother about the hapax legomena and her father's work on the subject. My mother leaned forward in her chair, her face bright and suddenly youthful.

Eva told her again about those words, which were found only once in the Bible. She explained how their meaning was often uncertain or fuzzy. The only way to determine what they might mean was through the context of the verse, but this, too, was often confusing. A better way to determine the precise meaning of a word was to compare it to similar words in the other ancient languages of the Near East, to Aramaic, Akkadian, Hittite, or the then recently discovered language of Ugaritic, first unearthed by archaeologists in northern Syria in 1929. Eva explained that all these ancient languages had many words derived from the same roots.

"Did your father know all those languages?" my mother asked in astonishment.

"Yes, Adele. Except for Ugaritic, which has only recently come to light. And that is my problem, which I will come to later. But first let me give you a few examples."

That evening around the sundial, Eva listed several hapax legomena to be found in the book of Genesis. She began with the word *copher*, the bitumen or pitch that Noah used to smear the ark before the flood and make it waterproof. "Bitumen is found in the Dead Sea," Eva told my mother. "In the language of Akkadians it was called *kupru*. It has all the same consonants when you take into account the differences in pronunciation."

"I didn't even know what bitumen meant in English!" my mother said.

Eva smiled and continued. There was the *"sulom,"* as in the verse about Jacob, *"Va'yachalom* . . . And he dreamed, and behold a *sulom* stood on earth and its head reached up to the heavens.

"The word *sulom* is usually translated as 'ladder.' Perhaps it means something else."

"But what else could it mean?" my mother asked Eva.

"A stairway, which is somewhat different from a ladder. In ancient times there were grand stairways in temples and palaces."

"Yes, of course, a grand stairway. What a lovely image. I never would have thought of that," my mother said. "And how do we know it?"

Eva told her of the myth of Sergal and Ereshkigal written in Akkadian and found on a series of tablets translated by a friend of her father's. In that story the divine messenger Namtar is said to ascend the long *s'l'm,* the "stairway" of heaven. And so *sulom* might better be translated as "stairway" rather than as "ladder."

My mother was delighted to be learning these strange and unusual things.

"You are a wonderful teacher with amazing things to teach," she told Eva. "It is so long since I've studied anything properly. I never finished college."

"I'll teach you whatever I can," Eva said. "I'm happy to do so."

"But what can I do for you in return?" my mother asked.

"You don't have to do anything, Adele. My only problem is there are new discoveries all the time, even now. I have

not been able to keep up all these years. I do not want my father's book to be out of date. Maybe if I need some books
and journals you can tell me where to get them. Are there
any libraries here?"

"Well, there is the public library."

Eva smiled. "Are there any university libraries?"

"There is a library at Assumption College. If they don't
have what you need we could go to Detroit or Ann Arbor."

"But I cannot cross the border."

"I could go for you, if you tell me what to look for."

"It's very easy. I can give you a list. There is something in
my father's manuscript about the Ugaritic language that I
do not understand. But I remember reading an article once
in the periodical *Orientalia*, or was it *Assyriology*? I think it
was in 1937 or 1938. Maybe they will have it at Assumption
College."

CHAPTER 18

ON THE MORNING OF THE SAB-
bath *Beha'alosekhoh,* I got up early to review the *parsha* before going to synagogue.
I sat in the kitchen so as not to wake anybody. Slowly, I read through the text twice
in a quiet voice.

As I was finishing, my mother and Asa
came into the kitchen. My mother wore a
black dress with a white bow at the neck
and a little black hat trimmed with black
beads.

Asa said, "Eva's still getting ready."

I went upstairs to put on my tie and
suit jacket, passing by Eva's room. The
door was wide open.

Eva stood facing the pier glass, her back

to the door, her feet, in black high heels with tips of gold, turned out ever so slightly. She wore a lavender and black patterned dress with elbow-length sleeves. She looked at my reflection in the mirror. She was adjusting a matching hat on her red hair. She carefully pulled the small black veil over her forehead and eyes.

She smiled. "Is it time to go yet?"

"Yes."

"I hope I haven't kept anyone waiting. I'm excited to hear you read, Joseph. It's been so long since I've been in a synagogue. It will be a great pleasure, I know."

She turned her head sideways, catching a lingering glimpse of herself in the mirror. "I'm ready now," she said.

On the porch, Asa stretched out his hand. Eva took it in hers. They stood for a moment framed by the trellis of Gracious Majesties. Here and there bees hovered around the flowers.

Eva took in a deep breath.

She said to the flowers, "Do not worry. I will not touch you today, it is the Sabbath."

This time I had the sensation that the roses were deliriously happy, that they had no fears or cares in the world. Their joy was transmitted to me. They knew they were abundant and luxurious and that everyone delighted in them and that this would protect them from harm.

Eva walked down the porch stairs, one foot placed

slowly and carefully in front of the other. The golden tips of her black shoes flashed and flickered.

"Have I told you about Solomon's bees?"

As we walked to synagogue Eva told us how the Queen of Sheba came to challenge King Solomon with riddles.

To test his wisdom, the Queen of Sheba dressed a thousand young maidens from her country in the most sumptuous clothes and then gave each one a bouquet of exquisitely fashioned artificial roses. These flowers were made with such remarkable craftsmanship that no one upon seeing them could tell the difference between them and real flowers.

Only one bouquet among the thousand was made of real roses.

The Queen of Sheba said, "I ask you, O wise King Solomon, to tell me which are the real flowers. All your armies and advisors will not be able to help you!"

King Solomon began to hum quietly as if he were merely thinking to himself, but actually he was summoning the bees, whose language he spoke and understood. All the bees in Jerusalem obeyed and came from their hives in the surrounding hills and valleys. They hovered in one great swarming pillar above the maiden who held the real roses.

King Solomon pointed. "There are my armies and there are my advisors. There, too, are your roses!"

The Queen of Sheba bowed to the ground. "All creatures are under your dominion and do your bidding. Will you teach your humble servant the language of the bees?"

King Solomon agreed and taught the Queen of Sheba

the language of the bees. The Queen of Sheba showed her gratitude. Eva quoted from the First Book of Kings:

" 'Va'teetayn l'melekh . . . And she gave the king one hundred and twenty talents of gold, and of spices very great store, and precious stones: there came no more such abundance as these which the Queen of Sheba gave to King Solomon. And so she turned and went to her own country, she and all her servants.'

"It is a true story, too," Eva told us. "I studied bees before I left Prague. They do have their own language."

When Eva finished speaking, we were standing in front of the synagogue.

MY READING from the Torah that Sabbath morning, my first one that summer, went without any "lasting errors." I caught the one pronunciation error I had made in the densely syntactic word v'ho'safsuf—"and the mixed multitude"—and corrected it. I felt this error would not count. It could not be held against me because I corrected it in time. I was very relieved.

In his sermon Rabbi Kremlach spoke of the week's parsha. He talked about the episode where Moses had asked Ḥovav, his father-in-law, who was also known as Jethro, to accompany the Children of Israel as they journeyed through the wilderness.

Moses said to his father-in-law, "Please do not leave us, because you know how we are to encamp in the wilderness and you shall be for us as eyes."

Rabbi Kremlach asked, "Why did Moses ask Ḥovav to be 'for us as eyes' when the Children of Israel had the glorious Pillar of Cloud to guide them?"

Rabbi Kremlach answered that Moses wanted to teach us that no matter how much we know, no matter how wise we think ourselves to be, we must always seek out those who can teach us something more, and as much knowledge and experience as possible. We must never feel we have enough knowledge and guidance.

At the end of his sermon Rabbi Kremlach said, "We'd like to thank Joseph for his excellent job reading the *parsha*. *Ashrei yoladitoh*—Happy is she who gave birth to him! We knew the son of Adele Ivri would not make too many mistakes. But Joseph made no mistakes at all!" Then the rabbi said, "We would like to welcome all the *ponim ḥadoshos*—the new faces in town. We hope everyone will welcome our guests in the social hall after services."

Though Rabbi Kremlach spoke in the plural, there was obviously only one newcomer in synagogue, Eva Higashi, who sat next to my mother in the women's section and whom he could see from the pulpit. She nodded in his direction.

In the social hall after services, everyone gathered around my mother and Eva. The two women towered above them all.

People began asking Eva questions all at once. She managed to answer with charm and consideration. Although her answers were brief, she made it seem as if she were giving all the time and attention in the world to each individual questioner.

Everyone was clearly fascinated by her, and this made me feel proud and uneasy at once.

"Where are you from?"

"You're staying with the Ivris?"

"How did you get here?"

"Really!"

"You couldn't go back?"

"Canadian immigration let you stay just like that? God bless Canada!"

"Oh, that Mr. Meadowlark. He smiles but he's a cruel one! He won't help anyone. He only takes advantage of people. He hates us!"

"These things are always for the best. You'll like Canada."

All this time no one said anything to me about my reading. They were so fascinated by Eva.

Rabbi and Isabel Kremlach came over as well.

Eva said, "I enjoyed your sermon very much, Rabbi. Perhaps Moses also knew that one day the Pillar of Cloud would leave and we would have to depend on our human understanding. My father believed that the Pillar of Cloud was also a symbol of living prophecy, which was later taken away from us."

For a moment Rabbi Kremlach was speechless. Finally he asked reverently, "Who was your father?"

"Enoch Laquedem."

"Yes, yes. I've read some of his work, years ago in seminary."

"Do you read German?" Eva asked.

"Not very well anymore. But I used to. Well, we usually do not have such interesting people in our synagogue. How is your father?"

"I do not know for sure. I am still looking for him, I'm afraid. I've tried to contact many people but I have not received any information."

"I'm sorry to hear that. I hope he is all right. My wife says you just came from Japan. You must forgive us all for being so curious."

"Not at all. That's the way it always is. But I suppose my new friends are tired. Joseph was up early to practice the reading. I must agree with you one hundred percent that he read flawlessly."

Isabel Kremlach whispered to me, "Why don't you bring your new boarder when you come to see Nebuchadnezzar?"

The way Isabel Kremlach said "your new boarder" bothered me. Eva was standing in front of her and she should have invited her herself. And she said nothing about my reading, which I worked hard to prepare.

Eva then turned to the small crowd that was lingering around her and the Kremlachs.

"It was a pleasure meeting all of you and especially hearing Joseph read so beautifully. I'm sorry we have to go now."

Despite Eva's pleasant voice, there was a distance and formality in her tone when she said this that I had not heard before.

As we walked home from synagogue, no one tried to approach or accompany us.

On our way my mother stopped for a moment to catch

her breath. She said to Eva, "What you said before about the Pillar of Cloud being a symbol of prophecy is interesting. It seems sad to me that we live now in a world without prophecy."

Eva said, "Yes, Adele, but all the old prophecies are in effect. And when something is taken from us we are always given something in its stead."

"What is that?"

"New forms of knowledge."

"I wish I knew the things you know, Eva."

"I do not know much, but I will teach you what I can."

Farther along our way home we took a street different from the one we came on. We passed a very old elm tree that Eva had not seen before.

She stood still for a moment to admire it.

"I always take the time to appreciate beauty whenever and in whatever form it might suddenly appear. My father always said, it is part of its nature, and God's will, for beauty to come along unexpectedly, to teach us by surprise."

"What does it teach us?" my mother asked.

Eva smiled. "Well, it is always something different. It makes us open our eyes. But what it teaches has nothing to do with Good and Evil. So we have to be very careful. Do you understand what I mean? It's a subtle distinction."

"I'm not sure I understand," my mother said. "I'm sorry. You must think I'm very simple."

Eva looked directly at my mother. "No. I do not, Adele. Please, you mustn't say that. Quite the contrary." She gently took my mother's arm. "But to answer your question, in the end, neither knowledge nor beauty makes a person good."

"Yes, that's true, Eva. I never thought of it that way," my mother said, and the two women walked arm in arm the rest of the way home.

THAT AFTERNOON I didn't go to see Nebuchadnezzar. I was still angry with Isabel for the way she said "your new boarder" and for saying nothing about my reading.

After the Sabbath was over, she called on the phone. "Are you feeling well, Joseph *muñeco*? Nebuchadnezzar was very worried. He was afraid you might be sick. I'm sure you've been busy preparing the *parsha* and helping your mother and the new boarder, but I hope you won't forget your old friends. Ruchi depends on you to take his place with Nebuchadnezzar while he is away."

CHAPTER 19

I KNEW RUCHI KREMLACH MY whole life, but did not consider him my "best friend" until I turned thirteen and he was fifteen, about a year before his parents had to send him away.

I did not have many friends and suddenly I began to think of Ruchi as my best friend now that he was paying some sort of vague attention to me and seemed willing to spend time together.

Ruchi was a good-looking boy with jet-black hair. He was very quiet and overly polite to adults, including my mother. My mother always said, "Ruchi is certainly very well brought up. He is very refined like his father."

Our sudden and brief friendship consisted of spending Sabbath or Sunday afternoons together at his house, quietly playing chess, which Ruchi enjoyed endlessly. When he sat concentrating at the chessboard, he pushed out his full lips, whistling softly to himself. Ruchi also liked to spend time looking at his stamp collection and adding to it. He carefully soaked and removed the stamps from the envelopes that arrived from his relatives in Cuba.

Sometimes, on sunny Sabbath afternoons, we went for walks to the Detroit River. For a long time Ruchi would be silent and then suddenly say, "My uncle owns two factories near Havana," or "My grandfather goes every day to sit at the beach near Miramar just like the old people do in Florida."

I would ask him questions: "Are you ever going to visit them?" or "What are your uncles like?"

"Someday I'll go to Havana. Without my parents, I hope. Then I'll get to know my uncles. Otherwise if my mother comes she will *charlar* nonstop and I won't be able to talk to them."

"Maybe they'll come here to visit one day," I said.

"Why would they want to do that?" Ruchi snapped.

Both Isabel and my mother were pleased with our new friendship since neither of us had many friends and we tended to be loners.

Isabel said, "I'm so glad you and Ruchi have become such good amigos. *¡Un amigo vale más que un amante!*—A friend is worth more than a lover!"

In the brief time of our friendship, before Ruchi was sent away, I noticed that his relationship with Nebuchadnezzar was deteriorating. One Sabbath afternoon, while we were walking to the river, Ruchi said angrily, "My mother thinks Nebuchadnezzar is a genius, she calls him *el gran genio* but he is only a stupid bird, like a chicken or a duck."

I was very upset to hear Ruchi speak against Nebuchadnezzar. I loved Nebuchadnezzar and, like Isabel, I believed he was an animal genius. I was ashamed of myself that I did not say anything in the parrot's defense, but I was afraid to provoke Ruchi. I worried, If Ruchi can turn against Nebuchadnezzar, who is like his brother and helped make it possible for him to be born, then maybe Ruchi will turn against me one day and stop being my friend, too. How could I depend on him? I discreetly tried to show extra interest in Nebuchadnezzar, hoping that Ruchi would care about him some more. If he realized his error then he would be less likely to repeat it with me. But this strategy only backfired on me. One day when he saw me talking to Nebuchadnezzar, he said, "Why are you talking to him so much? I told you he's a stupid bird. Only stupid people talk to stupid birds."

Soon Ruchi underwent other changes. He began to do poorly in school. He had always been an A student. One day I heard Isabel say to him, "Don't forget to finish reading the book for your book report."

He snapped back, "Shut up, you *bruja*!"

At first Isabel Kremlach would laugh nervously at Ruchi's changing behavior and later say to me, "Well, Ruchi is just finding his own way. He's just going through his rebellious phase. Lots of boys do. It doesn't mean anything.

My brother was like that, too, and, *mira*, Joseph, now he runs two factories, one for clothes and one for dress shoes!"

The last time I saw Ruchi was the Sabbath afternoon after Passover. It was a warm spring day and I hoped we might go for a walk to the river.

I came over to the Kremlachs' house. The front door was unlocked even though there had been several robberies in Windsor recently. Isabel had said we should all be more careful and lock our doors.

I knocked and then let myself in.

I heard loud voices and it took me a moment to make out what was being said.

"Who did such a terrible thing! Who did such a terrible thing! Ruchi, did you do that?!" Isabel was standing in the dining room. "How could you? Are you jealous of a bird? *¿Te volviste loco?*"

Rabbi Kremlach was standing there, too. His face was white. He spoke in barely a whisper. "Yeruchem Kremlach, what have you done?"

No one seemed to notice that I had walked into the dining room. I could not imagine what "terrible thing" might have happened. I was very scared nevertheless. There was an awful odor in the room.

Then I saw Nebuchadnezzar perched on the chandelier, panting. He flew off and circled the room, agitated. He hit his head on a windowpane. He landed on the dining room table and stood there for a moment stunned.

His brilliant feathers were somehow different.

They were smeared with something brown.

Next I saw Nebuchadnezzar's cage on the carpet. Something was in the floor of his cage. It took me a moment to figure out what it was.

Inside Nebuchadnezzar's cage was a pile of smashed brown turds. These were clearly human or dog feces, not bird feces. Ruchi just stood there, smiling strangely. He did not notice me at all.

"Answer me, Ruchi. Who did such a terrible thing?" Isabel repeated, the strength drained from her voice.

Ruchi then picked the cage from the carpet and shook it over the sofa. He laughed loudly, tossed the cage on the floor, and walked slowly out of the room.

The Kremlachs stood there. Isabel's shoulders sank. Finally Isabel realized I was there. Without looking directly at me, she said quietly, "I think you'd better go home now, Joseph."

The next day Ruchi was sent away to a hospital in St. Thomas.

Later in the week Isabel came over to our house. She spoke privately with my mother in the kitchen. She then came out and asked me to go for a little walk with her. I could tell she had been crying though she had tried to hide this.

Isabel said to me, "You are a sweet and kind boy, Joseph *muñeco*. Ruchi is just going through a difficult time now. But he will be back soon to his old self in no time at all. You can be sure of that.

"It's not people's business what happened. People are

not always so nice. They like to think the worst of others. Did you tell anyone besides your mother?"

I shook my head. How could I have told anyone? It was too terrible to tell. Ruchi had gone crazy and I had been his best friend.

Isabel's eyes filled with tears. "Of course, I knew you wouldn't, Joseph. You are such a good boy. You are Ruchi's best friend and will always protect his good name."

CHAPTER 20

HE DAY AFTER THE SABBATH *Beha'alosekhoh*, my mother said, "Wouldn't it be nice, Joseph, to show Eva around the county? The countryside is so pretty this time of year. We should show it to her. I don't have any baking to do today."

This sounded like a good idea to me. After all, Eva had said, "I always like to get to know the place I'm living in," and quoted from the Book of Numbers, " '*U're'isem* . . . And you shall see the land, what it is, and the people that dwelleth therein!' "

My mother even suggested an entire itinerary.

We could drive to Leamington, then to Point Pelee, a triangle of land that jutted out into Lake Erie. We could have a picnic on the beach. On our way home we could stop at the county fair, which was being held at Kingston.

Normally my mother did not like driving unless it was a short and familiar distance. Other cars on the road made her nervous. If the weather was bad, even if the sky was simply overcast, she would not drive the car at all. Although my father had been dead for three years she still called the small Austin Martin "your father's car."

Once, shortly after he died, I said to my mother, "It's not his car anymore."

She looked at me a moment. "No, Joseph. It is still your father's car."

At first when she started her baking business I had to run to the market or make small deliveries by bicycle, mostly to old people like Shooshy Kalkstein and her brother Maurice, who lived by the river. Other customers would simply come to the house and pick up their orders. Now with my mother's catering business growing she had to drive more often. The things she now needed to buy at the market or bring to the synagogue were too heavy for me to carry in my bicycle basket. "I cannot wait until you are old enough to drive, Joseph!" she said.

After my mother made her proposal about taking Eva around the county, she added, "Eva is teaching me so much and she has only been here a few days. I never knew any of the things she knows. And she's going to teach me more. Everything is so much nicer since she's been here. Just think, Asa's been out every day, and we haven't even had a single day of bad weather. Perhaps we should give Eva credit for that, too!"

My mother then began to repeat herself, which was unusual for her and made me uncomfortable. Again she said, "The countryside is so pretty this time of year. We should show it to her." She then hesitated. "Do you think, Joseph . . . do you think maybe Eva will really want to stay with us for . . . for a long time?"

I said I thought so.

But the question bothered me. My mother usually spoke with assurance. Now I could not stop thinking about this new hesitation in my mother's voice.

How could I know if Eva would stay? Why was my mother asking me? I thought of the verse I had read in synagogue and that Eva had quoted when she picked up my *tiykun: Would that all God's people were prophets.*

I was not a prophet. I could not tell the future.

I felt a new and unbearable pressure, as if Eva's staying or going depended on me. I had the idea, too, that the reason I felt compelled to read all the *parshios* every week was that if I hadn't, Eva would not have come to us. I tried to calculate back in time to the actual day that Rabbi Kremlach had asked me to be *ba'al koreh.* I figured out that weeks before, at the very moment when Rabbi Kremlach asked me to fill in for Mr. Zubrovsky, and I agreed, Eva's destiny was changed. The coincidence was amazing. At that very moment when I said yes to Rabbi Kremlach, Eva set sail on the *Jewel of the Seas.* This in turn set into motion all the subsequent events that brought her to us. Perhaps my continued readings were needed, not to prevent bad things from happening, but to cause the good things to remain and even more good things to happen.

I had the sudden idea that if ever I made a mistake in the reading, Eva would be forced to leave. This was an alarming realization for me and brought with it the need for an elaborate analysis of the possibilities. I came to the temporarily reassuring conclusion that the fatal mistake would be not just any mistake, but a certain mistake I could not foresee, lying in wait there for me like the mouth of the earth that was prepared at Creation to swallow up the wicked Koraḥ in his rebellion against the authority of Moses. I tried to reassure myself and told myself that if the mistake was caught right away, this terrible punishment would not apply. Only if I made the mistake and no one, not even my mother, caught it in time.

But this convoluted reassurance did not last long. I thought to myself, How could I help not making a great mistake from time to time? A mistake that even my mother might not catch. It would be an impossible feat to be perfect. Eventually I was doomed. But how could it be my fault? And why should Eva leave us just for that?

These thoughts began to overwhelm me and in an attempt to make them go away I began to practice even harder. This meant I had less time for myself but still I tried to go with Eva on her various outings. In the coming days and weeks I began to sleep poorly and would wake up in the middle of the night and practice some more. I was very tired during the day. It occurred to me that I might be going crazy like Ruchi.

E va was delighted by my mother's proposal. "I would love to see the countryside, Adele."

"I hope I'm not distracting you from your work."

"I can take one morning off from work. I've delayed so much already. I'm not concentrating so well today anyway. I could use a little change of scenery."

Asa made a suggestion to Eva. "You should see the whole area first so you get the big picture. Joseph, can we show her where we live in the *Atlas of Canada?*"

I brought the heavy book to the sunroom, where we all sat around Eva. I opened it to the page where the peninsula of southern Ontario is shown extending down between Lake Huron on one side and lakes Erie and Ontario on the other.

"It looks like a wonderful bird diving into the water," Eva said.

She then took out her magnifying glass.

Her long thin neck curved ever so slightly as she inclined her head downward. She, too, reminded me of an elegant, exotic bird as she peered at the map.

With her red fingernail, magnified under the glass, she traced the waterways that flowed past Windsor and eventually out across the entire world.

Her magnified fingernail fascinated me. The shape of the nail, even under such scrutiny, seemed perfect and the skin on the finger so smooth and pale as it glided along the blue surface of the waterways.

Carefully, as if she were designing the waterways herself, she followed the Detroit River as it flowed into Lake Erie, which in turn connected to Lake Ontario. From Lake Ontario she traced the St. Lawrence Seaway to the Atlantic Ocean. She turned through the pages and outlined a route through the seas and oceans covering the earth.

"See, you could travel the entire world from here, all the way to China." She pointed to the map. "Did I tell you I traveled often to Shanghai? See? Here it is right on the mouth of the Yangtze River. My husband was posted there during the war. It's a very cosmopolitan city with people from all over the world. I visited him several times."

THAT AFTERNOON, my mother and Eva sat in the front seat. I sat with Asa in the back. Asa kept all the windows open. It was very sunny. Asa wore his sunglasses and the silk veiling over his face.

Asa announced a new game, Blind Man in a Car.

"That's terrible, Asa," my mother said. "You are not blind."

Asa insisted on his game. "I'm practicing for when I'm blind."

Asa said he could tell where we were going, even with his eyes closed. He sat very still, alert to the sounds and smells, trying to feel every turn of the car. My mother had not taken the most direct route out of Windsor but wanted to show Eva different parts of the city.

Asa said, "We're driving east along the river. I can tell by the smell of the water. It smells stinky."

My mother slowed the car. "You still see very well, Asa. The doctor said you might see well for many years to come. You are only ten years old. You have your whole life ahead of you. What do you think, Eva?"

Eva said, "I have to agree with your mother, Asa.

"Did you know that when I was still studying in the university I studied the vision of bees? Did you know bees can see all sorts of colors? They can see some colors that we cannot."

"What colors?"

"Colors we cannot even guess at. They can see ultra-violet—"

Asa interrupted, "Now we are going south over the road that will take you to Toronto where the doctors are in the Middle Ages and cannot do anything. They have the biggest and dumbest hospital in the world. They could not make my father better. And I'm sure they don't know anything about silk."

My mother said, "Well, it doesn't matter what the doctors can and cannot do. They don't have all the answers. You have to trust in Hashem, Asa. He sent us Eva so you would learn about silk. Just when you needed to. And it isn't polite to interrupt."

Eva closed her eyes. "I shall play a game, too. My game is

called If We Were in Prague. It goes like this. If we were in Prague and strolling along the river, then we would be seeing the Hradčany Castle on the other side! Try to imagine it!"

I had no idea what the Hradčany Castle might look like. Still I tried, as Eva had asked, to imagine it. I pictured in my mind a colorful castle like one I had seen in a storybook. For a moment this conjured edifice on the other side of the Detroit River with its flagged towers and banner-festooned turrets seemed vivid to me.

"Do you miss your home very much, Eva?" my mother asked.

My imaginary castle vanished.

"I miss Prague very much, Adele. Last night I dreamed I was in my father's study again and Asa was sitting with him, reading his books!"

I felt a sudden shock, since this was just like the dream I had the night Eva came to live with us in which Eva's father and Asa were reading from the Midrash on Evening Faces. I remembered the powerful longing I had felt because I was not able to remember what the Midrash taught us.

Now I felt agitated that Eva had dreamed of Asa. Why not of me? Weren't dreams the things you were thinking about that day? She must have been thinking of her father and Asa, the people she loved.

"Eva, would you rather go back to Prague than be with us in Windsor?" Asa asked.

Eva paused. "Well, I can only be exactly where I am, so that is where I'm meant to be. And I cannot go back anymore."

"Why?"

"Because everything has changed. There is no freedom. And anyway I am happy to be here with you."

WE HAD DRIVEN WEST before turning south. Asa had guessed wrong initially. We rounded the toe of our peninsula and eventually did head east to Leamington.

When we entered the town we saw a huge, story-high red tomato that served as an information booth and tourist attraction. On top was a sign that said, "Welcome to the Tomato Capital of the World."

"The fruit of this land is mighty!" Eva said.

We all laughed.

"I have never eaten a tomato."

We had never heard anything so ridiculous.

"You never even had ketchup?" Asa asked.

"No. What is ketchup?"

"Dead squished tomatoes. I don't like ketchup," Asa said.

"I don't think I will like ketchup either!"

We drove to Point Pelee, where we had a small picnic at a beach table.

On our way back, near Kingston, we stopped at the county fair, which had an amusement park. Asa and I went on several rides while my mother and Eva watched. When it came time to go on the Ferris wheel, Eva said she wanted to go, too. Asa and I climbed into a car and my mother and Eva got into the one behind us. At the top of the Ferris wheel, I turned around and saw my mother lifting up her hands to cover her face.

Eva gently put her arm around my mother's shoulder.

"Joseph, you're crushing me!" Asa screamed.

"I'm sorry," I said. "It was an accident."

"No, it wasn't! You did it on purpose."

"I said I was sorry."

My mother did not put her hands down until the ride was over. Later she said, "I never used to be afraid of heights."

After the Ferris wheel, we walked by the Tunnel of Love.

"Oh, that looks like fun and not too dangerous," my mother said, laughing.

"Yes, why don't we all go?" Eva said.

Asa did not want to go in. It was dark inside and he would not be able to see. He waited outside with my mother.

I sat in a gondola seat with Eva.

"Isn't this exciting?" Eva said to me. Her long legs were cramped and squeezed next to mine. I felt the fragrant warmth of her body. I inhaled deeply.

Suddenly I felt so happy.

Our little gondola jerked from side to side as we floated through the Tunnel of Love. Scattered in its dark firmament, little hearts twinkled like stars. Romeo and Juliet glowed and kissed on the walls.

Eva pointed to a smiling crescent moon where a rocking cupid sat taking aim.

"He looks like Asa!" she said, as we floated out into the sunlight.

ON THE WAY HOME we took a different, convoluted route. We drove past the Kalkstein house. It sat on the edge of the Detroit River with a fine view. It had become more dilapidated since Maurice and Shooshy died. Before the house stood two grand trees that always flowered in the spring. They had been planted in the previous century. They were the only two of their kind in town, being rare in our part of the world. The trees were past their bloom. I had always admired them but until that day I had not known their name.

Eva said, "How wonderful. Paulownia trees are my favorite trees. There is a magnificent one in the garden of the Hradčany Castle where my father used to take me. These two are almost as beautiful. I wish I could see them bloom." She quoted from the words of Balaam, who gazed upon the Children of Israel spread out before him in the wilderness:

> "'K'n'halim nitayu . . . As the valleys stretched out
> As the gardens by the riverside;
> As aloe trees which the Lord has planted,
> As the cedars beside the waters.'"

"Eva," my mother said. "You make the words of the Torah come to life!"

"You know, if I were rich again I would buy a house on the river."

"You were rich?" Asa asked.

"When I was growing up in Prague, I had everything I needed. If you have everything you need, then you are rich."

IT WAS TWILIGHT when we parked in front of our house. Hundreds of fireflies began rising from the grass, even more than I had seen that first evening when Eva arrived, when I had watched her moving in her room from our backyard garden.

"It's magical," my mother said.

"What's like magic?" Asa asked.

"The fireflies," I said.

Asa began to cry. "I can't see them!"

"Come with me, Asa," Eva said. "Would you find my magnifying glass, Joseph?"

She gave me her handbag. I felt for the magnifying glass and pulled it out. My hand brushed against the lacquerware box, which held the *Augsburg Miscellany.*

Eva walked carefully in her high-heel shoes on the grass. She bent over and caught a firefly in her hand.

"Let's look under the lens."

I held the magnifying glass over the small opening she made in her cupped fist. The moon had risen full overhead.

"Can you see it now, Asa?" she asked. "Can you see it under the glass?"

"Oh, yes, Eva," he said with a slight trembling in his voice. "Yes, I see it. Look, how it sparkles."

She released the firefly and with a smile took her handbag back from me and slung it over her shoulder. As we walked up the porch steps I noticed Eva twisting her diamond ring. Perhaps she had turned the jewel inward when she cupped her hands together, making Asa think he was actually seeing a firefly.

I did not know if Asa really saw the faint glow of the firefly in Eva's palm, even with the magnifying glass, or if he had actually seen her diamond, or perhaps the magnifying glass itself, somehow catching and reflecting moonlight. But it did not matter. I already knew she had the power to make us see castles and magical giraffes that weren't there.

THAT NIGHT, before we went to bed, Eva thanked my mother for the wonderful day.

"It was my pleasure, Eva. I enjoyed myself, too."

"Maybe tomorrow I will go to Assumption College and look for that article I mentioned the other evening."

"That's an excellent idea."

The next day Asa and I walked with Eva to the library at Assumption College. They did not carry *Orientalia* or *Assyriology*, the journals Eva needed.

When we returned home, Eva said to my mother, "I don't know what I will do, Adele. It is so important to have the right materials."

"Don't worry, Eva. I told you before I could go to Detroit. I will go tomorrow."

"You are so good to me, Adele!" Eva kissed my mother on the cheek.

My mother blushed.

And so my mother, who had never liked driving unless it was a short and familiar distance, began to put away her fears. She had already surprised me by driving around to show Eva the countryside, and now she happily began driving once or twice a week to the library at Wayne State University to help Eva with her research.

CHAPTER 21

E XCEPT DURING THE YEAR OR TWO
after his wife abandoned him and his
daughter, Enoch Laquedem wrote prolifically. He produced dozens of essays and
monographs on a wide range of topics
from history to Midrashic commentaries,
to comparative linguistics, including the
hapax legomena, which Eva had taught
my mother that summer in the evenings
around the garden sundial. He had been
particularly excited by the reports following the discovery of the Ugaritic texts in
1929, which had slowly begun to be published in the next decade.

Many of Enoch Laquedem's works had
appeared in respected scholarly journals or

tiny academic presses, and found their way into small and large libraries around the world, even if sometimes in the most remote and obscure stacks. I realized this from the summer Eva stayed with us and my mother found such journals as the *Biblische Monatsschrift, Orientalia,* and *Assyriology* in the library of Wayne State University.

Over the course of decades, I have found many other articles written by Laquedem. I have searched the many *Wissenschaft* journals of the time, some of which are now obscure and hard to find. I have gone through their contents carefully, reading the various articles that interest me just as my mother researched the journals at Wayne State University to see if there was anything of interest to Eva, even though she did not understand very much German.

It was through the prodding of Dr. Schpizhof that I myself studied German and improved the French I had learned in school growing up in Canada.

Several years ago I found Laquedem's monograph *Midrash, Metaphor, and Prophecy* in the library of the Jewish Museum in Prague. At the beginning Laquedem quotes the verse that Eva recited to us that first day she came into our house and picked up my *tiykun: Would that all God's people were prophets.*

In a lengthy discussion, Laquedem put forth the bold theory that the imaginative, cross-referencing commentaries of the Midrash were meant to replace Biblical prophecy:

The loss of the true prophets and their prophecy was for post-biblical society in Palestine perhaps their greatest tragedy, more so than the physical destruction of the Temple or the political loss of Jerusalem. How were they to replace that intangible and sacred institution?

Before answering this question, Laquedem gave his definition of what constitutes prophecy.

The mere prediction of future events is a rather simplistic and insufficient definition of prophecy. The real intent of prophecy and the mission of the prophets is to teach us how to live in the present world, to see the holy patterns and make sense of its endless confusions.

Laquedem proposed that the divine inspiration with which prophets always speak is in reality an understanding of what he termed *das Netz der Wirklichkeit*—the net of reality.

It is this "net of reality" which weaves seemingly disparate things together and makes of them whole cloth. On its own our world seems a chaos of unrelated events to the human mind, but in fact this is not the case. This perception is only due to our limitations of observation and reason. Prophecy and the intellectual tools of the sages who composed the Midrashic commentaries are an attempt to find order and connection so that some sense can be made of our world. But we must be careful, too, in such analyses. Such efforts can be a dangerous pursuit. Like those scientists in our time who try fruit-

lessly to find the spirit which resides in the material brain, one cannot dissect such a delicate and phantom-like creature as prophecy without causing its death.

Although I have spent the last decades searching for everything Laquedem wrote, I have never found what I was really looking for.

I have never found a copy of *Clouds of Glory* or any evidence that it was ever published after Eva left our home.

CHAPTER 22

VA LAQUEDEM MET CHUJO HIGASHI
when both were studying at the Charles
University in Prague.

Chujo had come from the city of Fukuoka on the island of Kyūshū to study at
the faculty of medicine. Eva was beginning
her studies at the faculty of science, taking
courses in chemistry, biology, and physics.

For a short while she worked with the
entomologist Dr. Penelope Kastner-Lublin,
a world authority on insect physiology.

It was in the laboratory of this scientist
that Eva met her future husband, due to
what might be one of the more peculiar
ideas that had floated among Japanese

military planners just before the beginning of the Second World War.

One day, several months before the Nazis invaded Czechoslovakia, Dr. Kastner-Lublin was visited by a delegation from the Japanese government.

For many years Kastner-Lublin, like the famous Dr. Karl von Frisch, had been studying the vision of bees and their ability to see light and colors in the short wavelength, ultraviolet range—light and colors that are invisible to us humans. Along with her extensive experiments with color perception, she began early investigations into another remarkable ability of these creatures, their ability to see polarized light, which humans and other vertebrates cannot, and their ability to navigate based on this perception. It had been observed that bees could navigate by the position of the sun even under a cloudy sky. In the 1930s Dr. Kastner-Lublin had published several papers, including "Alterations of Light Polarization in Various Atmospheric Phenomena and the Perception of Bees," and "A Microscopic Study of the Ommatidium (Eye Organ) of the Honey Bee."

At that time the Japanese military began to invest in an array of seemingly unusual scientific research projects and were interested in this example of advanced insect reconnaissance, hoping that with further study they might somehow be able to apply certain principles to their army and air force. Dr. Kastner-Lublin's research was highly sophisticated and involved an understanding not only of bee visual systems and neurophysiology but the physics of light in the polarized state.

The Japanese had come to her laboratory on a pretext, to see if she would be at all sympathetic to their country's well-being. They asked if she would be willing to help them investigate a new disease that was threatening the silkworm population in Japan. In this way, they reminded her, Dr. Kastner-Lublin was not unlike Louis Pasteur, who had been approached by the French government in the previous century to investigate the silkworm disease known as pébrine.

Chujo Higashi, whose family owned mills and filatures in Fukuoka and had connections to the military, was fluent in German. His government asked that he join the small Japanese delegation, although he did not actually speak at the meeting or address Dr. Kastner-Lublin.

Eva was in the laboratory when the delegation arrived.

Penelope Kastner-Lublin politely listened to the delegation's request and then just as politely turned them down.

"I am very sorry I cannot help you. I have spent my life studying the vision of bees. I know nothing about the lepidoptera and their diseases."

"But perhaps the distinguished Madame Professor might give more thought to helping us," the leader of the delegation said. "The silk moths and their larvae are insects after all. It is a grave threat to our economy and therefore to the well-being of our people."

"I am sorry about your difficult situation, but moths are simply not the same as bees," the entomologist said firmly.

"Perhaps, Madame will take some days to reconsider. These are such unsettled times. If you came to work for us in Japan, we would be certain to take good care of you and provide you with all your needs. You could continue to work on your bees."

She thought for a long moment. "No. No. I am sorry I cannot be of service. I do not wish to waste any more of anyone's time. I have several daylight experiments to do. It will soon be dark outside. Miss Laquedem, will you please escort the gentlemen out."

THAT EVENING someone knocked at the Laquedem apartment on Pařížká Street.

Eva answered the door.

She recognized the young man from the delegation. He was holding a book in his hands, his fingers obscuring the title.

He bowed his head in greeting.

"My name is Chujo Higashi. You are Miss Laquedem."

"Yes, that's true. May I help you?"

"Do you really love insects?"

She smiled. "Yes, very much."

"Do you like fireflies?"

"I do not know much about them. Are the fireflies in your country sick, too?"

He laughed. "No, not at all. That would be a great catastrophe! Do you know our *Tale of Genji?*"

She did not.

"It is a wonderful story. Here it is." He handed her the book he was holding.

Eva opened the book and laughed. "Thank you, but I cannot read Japanese."

"That does not matter. One day I shall read for you the chapter called 'Fireflies.' Unfortunately there is no chapter on bees to entertain you with."

"Would you read it to me in Japanese?" Eva asked.

"Would you like to learn it? I would be honored to teach you."

"I will look forward to that."

"When shall we start our lessons?"

"Whenever you are ready."

"I am ready now."

CHUJO AND EVA began to see each other. He would pick her up at the laboratory in the evenings after work and they would walk through the city, each time along different streets.

Wherever they walked, something reminded Chujo of Fukuoka, although the cities were so different from each other.

The Vltava River reminded Chujo Higashi of the more modest Naka River that divided his hometown. Hradčany Castle reminded him of the Fukuoka Castle. And when Eva showed him her beloved paulownia tree in the Hradčany Castle gardens, Chujo was reminded of the famous Tobiume, the Flying Plum Tree on the grounds of the Dazaifu Shrine. He told Eva the legend of this loyal tree, which jumped from the city of Kyoto to follow the scholar Sugawara Michizane when he was exiled to the island of Kyūshū. Its blossoms had always been Michizane's favorite flower.

Eva would smile and take his hand. "You are infected with nostalgia, Chujo!"

"I suppose so. Perhaps it is because I am so troubled."

Chujo Higashi could not help worrying about the dangerous course his country was now taking.

The day came when Eva, too, would be filled with an unending nostalgia for her own home.

"Now, I am sorry for teasing him," she told us. "But he always took it with good nature. My husband never did adjust to Prague."

S O O N A F T E R the invasion of Czechoslovakia, Dr. Kastner-Lublin's laboratory was ransacked. Dr. Kastner-Lublin disappeared. Eva could not find out whether she had been arrested or had somehow escaped the country.

In time Eva was no longer allowed to attend the university.

"Marry me," Chujo said to her on the Charles Bridge. "You can leave right away for Japan. You will be safe there. I will come to you soon."

S H E B A D E a tearful goodbye to her father at the train station, on the very first leg of her journey, which would

take her to Moscow and from there across Siberia to Vladivostok.

"That was the last time I saw my father," Eva told us. "He
was standing next to Chujo on the platform."

Several months later Chujo Higashi finished his medical
studies and joined his European wife in Japan.

CHAPTER 23

ONE AFTERNOON, A FEW WEEKS after Eva began sending telegrams all over the world, a yellow cab pulled up in front of our house. Two men got out, one old, one young. Although it was a hot day, they both wore black suits and black hats. The older man had a long gray beard. The younger had a trim blond beard and was very thin.

I went to open the door. As the men walked up the porch stairs, their black figures were framed in the brilliant red of the roses.

My mother joined me in the front hall. She whispered to me, "It must be a mistake, Joseph. They probably want to see

Rabbi Kremlach to raise money for their yeshiva. Maybe you can take them there."

The men stood before the threshold and politely introduced themselves.

"We were sent, Madame, by the Amitzer Rebbe, who has recently settled in Jerusalem. We have come to see Eva Marie Laquedem of Prague. The Rebbe received a telegram from her. It was sent to the wrong country but fortunately it was forwarded to the Rebbe immediately. We have been traveling in America. The Rebbe has contacted us and asked us to see her and find out how she is. We hope we have not missed her. She is still here, isn't she?"

"Yes. She's staying with us," my mother said. "But her name is Mrs. Higashi now." Then she added softly, as if to explain and excuse to these devout gentlemen the reason for Eva's marriage to a Japanese, "Her late husband saved her life."

The two men glanced at each other. "Yes, he has done a great deed. Would you tell Mrs. Higashi that we are here?"

My mother showed them into the living room. She offered them seats, but they preferred to wait standing.

My mother went upstairs to get Eva. That afternoon Eva had taken a break from her father's book to give Asa one of his lessons in calligraphy. In fact, she did not teach him true calligraphy but rather the drawing of various Japanese pictograms in pencil. Sometimes I would take a few moments from my practicing to watch them.

Eva would draw carefully on a piece of paper. "This is the symbol for tree—木, and this is the symbol for the sun—日. If you show the sun rising behind a tree in the morning, you get this pictograph— 東 —which means 'east.'

"Do you boys know how to say 'east' in Japanese?"

We did not.

"Higashi!"

WHILE THE EMISSARIES were waiting for my mother to get Eva, they asked me several questions:

How old was I?

Did I read Hebrew?

Did I learn Torah every day?

I told them I was reading every week in synagogue while the *ba'al koreh* was away.

This news pleased them.

They asked me to recite for them. I was nervous but picked up my *tiykun*. I read the verse from that week's portion where I had just left off practicing.

"'*Va'yiru kol ho'aydoh* . . . And all the congregation saw that Aaron was dead, and they wept for Aaron thirty days, all the house of Israel.'"

The younger man said, "Very good, Yosef. The words will stay with you your whole life."

The older man seemed to be hesitating and finally said, "It must be pleasant to have Mrs. Higashi living in your house. She is a very educated woman, no? A scientist?"

"Yes, she is," I said. "She knows Hebrew and the Torah, too. I think her father taught her."

This made them smile.

Just then, Eva came down the stairs followed by my mother and Asa.

When they saw her, the emissaries bowed their heads respectfully.

Eva bowed her head in return. She smiled, holding her hands modestly in front of her. They did not shake hands. Her bag hung over her shoulder on its strap. She made a short greeting in a strange language, perhaps Czech.

She then switched to English.

"I am grateful to your Rebbe for having sent you," she said. "My father always spoke highly of him. They shared many ideas although they had such different philosophies."

"The Rebbe has always held your father's wisdom in the greatest esteem."

Until that moment they had all been standing. Eva motioned them to take their seats in the two armchairs. I sat next to Eva on the sofa.

Asa looked at the two men, shrugged, and decided to go outdoors to play.

"Don't worry, I'll put on my silk," he told Eva.

"That's a good idea, Asa. It's a sunny day."

"I'll practice my new pictogram later."

"Good, Asa."

My mother offered the men something to eat, perhaps a piece of cake she had just baked. They politely declined the cake. Although they did not mention it, they would not eat anything my mother had baked. They did not know her and could not trust the ritual strictness of her kitchen.

Eva said to my mother, "Perhaps the gentlemen would like fruit and some ice water or juice. Though I don't mean to trouble you, Adele."

"Oh, yes, yes," my mother said, understanding Eva's hint that these things would be permissible to the emissaries.

The men politely declined even this offer.

"Well, then, I'll leave you alone with your visitors," my mother said. "If you need me I will be in the kitchen. I have more cakes in the oven."

She turned to me, "Joseph, I'm sure Eva would like to talk with her visitors privately."

"Oh, no," Eva said. "I would be grateful to Joseph if he would stay. Perhaps he can help me if I need anything." She looked at the emissaries. "I'm sure the men will have no objections."

They seemed to hesitate but deferred to Eva. "He is a learned and intelligent boy. He reads the Torah very well."

This remark pleased my mother and put her at ease. She said, "Well, if you will excuse me, I'll get back to my work," though I think that she, too, wanted to hear what the men had to say.

The older man said, "The Rebbe was happy to receive your telegram. He did not know what became of you. The Rebbe has always been grateful to you and your father for all you have done for his family."

"I was hoping the Rebbe might have news of my father. I have not heard from my father in all these years. He knew where to find me had he been able to. I am still searching for him."

The two men looked at each other.

Eva's voice rose slightly.

"I am prepared to hear the truth. I have been waiting a long time for the truth." Without looking at me, she took hold of my hand. I was surprised by this gesture and blushed. I felt the cool metal of her ruby bracelet brush my wrist. I felt ashamed of my hand. It was thin and bony and sweaty, but I stayed perfectly still while Eva's warm dry hand gripped mine tightly.

The older man spoke slowly. "I am very sorry. The Rebbe has had a report, which is several years old but reliable. He heard it from one of his disciples. Your father was taken to the Terezín ghetto outside Prague."

"When?"

"In the winter of 1944."

Eva sat very straight on the sofa. "What happened to him? Was he sent on to the camps?"

"No. At first he was put on the Council of Elders, that is how the Rebbe's disciple even heard of him. He did not know him personally. They never met. There had even been a rumor that one of the council members was to be released and sent to Switzerland. But it wasn't true."

The man hesitated.

Eva gripped my hand even harder. "Please go on."

"Your father was hanged."

Eva pressed her other hand to her chest.

There was a silence and then Eva said, "Go on. I want to know everything."

"Your father was hanged in public with two other council members. On the first day of Passover in the main ghetto square. I'm sorry. We do not know why. The murderers did not need any reason to kill."

The man hesitated again.

"The bodies were left hanging for three days."

Eva mumbled something.

I could not tell what she was saying or in what language.

Her hand became clammy and released mine. She slumped back onto the sofa, her mouth open.

"She fainted!" the men said.

I ran and got my mother.

She directed the two men to lay Eva flat on the sofa.

Although they were not permitted to touch a woman not their wife, and did not shake hands with Eva when they arrived, the men did as my mother instructed. It was an emergency and so they were obligated.

"Eva! Wake up! Wake up!" My mother patted her lightly on both cheeks.

She turned to the men. "What happened?"

"Her father was killed. It is already several years."

"Poor Eva! Joseph, get me some cold water."

I ran to the kitchen. I was shaking terribly and it seemed it would take forever to find a glass and turn on the faucet. I had never seen anyone faint and it appeared a very serious thing.

When I returned to the living room, Asa appeared.

"Eva's dead! I knew it! Everyone dies in this house! Everybody dies in this house!"

"Calm yourself, Asa," my mother said. I could not remember my mother speaking to him so sternly. "Calm yourself this minute, Asa Ivri. Eva will be fine."

Asa stood silently in his place like a little statue.

Eva began to rouse herself. She opened her eyes.

"Are you all right, Eva?" my mother said.

She nodded.

The emissaries said, "We are sorry to have been the messengers of such terrible news."

Eva said weakly, "No, you had to tell me. It was your duty. How could you not? I needed to know. Not knowing has been a torment."

She slowly sat up. She took in a deep breath. She pulled on the collar of her dress until it tore.

Eva's eyelids fluttered and she looked like she might faint again.

My mother said, "I will call Dr. Fairclough."

"No," Eva said. "These men have come a long way and . . . just let me shut my eyes." She closed her eyes again.

"Your father was a brave man, Mrs. Higashi. At the beginning of the war your father helped save the Rebbe and his wife. He was able to bribe some officials, we believe with things that had come to the museum there. The Rebbe never found out what exactly. Your father was able to keep secrets under the worst circumstances.

"The Rebbe wishes to tell you that if you are ever in need of anything at all, you must ask him. If it is in his power it will be done."

Eva waved her hand. She did not seem to be concentrating anymore. "Yes, yes. Thank you. I'm . . . I'm very tired now. Will you excuse me? I need to lie down."

Although she was distraught and had just fainted, I noticed she did not cry, just as, years before, I did not cry at my father's death. I could not help thinking over and over, Yes, we are the same somehow. We are the same. This is how people of the world behave. Eva and I are the same somehow.

Eva got up and went toward the stairs. My mother joined her, putting her arm around her narrow waist.

The emissaries stood up.

Eva suddenly turned to them.

"How is the Rebbe's granddaughter, Rachel?"

"Rachel is married now. She lives in B'nei Brak just outside Tel Aviv. She married the Tamimer Rebbe's son. They have two little boys."

"And her eyesight? How is her eyesight?"

They shook their heads. "She is practically blind. But God looks after her. She is a fine woman. She manages very well. She has often spoken of you and your kindness. She has not forgotten."

Eva nodded. "I'm glad to hear that. Very glad. She was a sweet girl. She had so much imagination."

Eva went up the stairs supported by my mother.

When the women were gone, the older man handed me a flat box.

"Please, Yosef, give this to Mrs. Higashi when she is feeling better. It is a gift from the Rebbe."

A WHILE LATER Dr. Fairclough arrived.

"She received a terrible shock," my mother was saying as they went upstairs.

When Dr. Fairclough entered Eva's room, he paused a moment. My mother had closed the drapes and the room was dark. Eva lay spread out on the bed, her eyes closed, on top of her orange-and-gold brocade cloth. Her red hair was undone.

"Eva, Eva," my mother whispered. "The doctor is here."

Eva opened her eyes. "Thank you, Adele."

Dr. Fairclough whispered something to my mother.

"Of course," she said. She escorted Asa and me out of the room, closing the door behind her.

On the way down the stairs Asa began whimpering. "She's going to die, isn't she?"

"No, Asa, she is not," my mother said. This time her voice was gentle, not stern. "Eva's not going to die. Don't worry. She has just heard some very sad news."

WHEN DR. FAIRCLOUGH came downstairs, he said to my mother, "It's a mild case of emotional shock, understandable under the circumstances. She just needs some rest and loving care, which I know you will provide, Adele.

"She is a charming young woman, Adele. It is hard to believe she has been through so much. Perhaps she needs some small distractions. Try to spend as much time with her as you can. I will check on her again tomorrow."

As Dr. Fairclough was leaving the house he added, "Maybe in a few days you should all come along for a ride on my boat. I think you might enjoy that."

"Thank you, Doctor."

That evening my mother knocked on Eva's door and brought her tea and a piece of cake.

"Thank you, Adele. This looks delicious."

Eva asked that we all come into her room to keep her company. She appeared in a happy mood again, even though earlier that same day she learned her father had been killed.

She sat on her bed and picked at her cake.

"I suppose I really knew all along. But I never wanted to admit it to myself." She looked pleadingly at my mother, the way Asa would plead with me. "It would have been wrong of me to give up hope without really knowing, wouldn't it?"

"You were right not to give up hope until now," my mother said.

"When I came here I remembered that the Rebbe had been friends with my father. I knew my father had been trying to help the Rebbe and his wife leave Prague. I do not know how he managed it in the end. He did not tell me. He must have sold things to raise the money. Our bank account in Prague was frozen."

"The men told me to give you this from their Rebbe." I handed Eva the box the emissaries had given me.

"How nice. Why don't we see what it is?"

She opened it slowly as she always would the lacquer-ware box. Inside was a thin book with a brown leather binding.

She pointed to her handbag. "Joseph, would you take out my white gloves?"

I searched inside and found her gloves. She put them on, then opened the pages of the book.

"Oh, this is lovely," Eva said softly. She was deeply moved. Her green eyes became moist and shone even more than usual. "A *Perek Shira*—a *Chapter of Song*. Do you know what it is?"

We did not.

She explained how the slender volume showed all of God's creation, the heavens and earth, animals and plants, singing praises to their Maker.

"The illustrations are lovely. I believe it must be Italian, maybe fifteenth century. Why don't you read from it, Adele?"

"Where should I start?"

"Anywhere."

My mother picked a paragraph illustrated with a picture of palm trees and a garden.

She read out loud:

"'*Gan Ayden omer* . . . The Garden of Eden says: Arise O North Wind and come south. Blow upon my garden that its fragrances flow out. Let my beloved come into his garden and eat its choicest fruits.'"

I blushed. Had Eva seen me walk in the gardens below her room in the dark evenings? Had she seen me spying in through her windows, even if it was only through the drawn curtains? Even if all I could see were shadows?

But Eva was concentrating on the manuscript with my mother.

LATER THAT EVENING my mother called Rabbi Kremlach to ask him a question of religious law.

He told her that since Eva had heard the news of her father's death several years after its occurrence she was not required to sit the usual week of shiva. Under these extraordinary circumstances she need only sit shiva for one hour.

CHAPTER 24

D R . FAIRCLOUGH DID NOT FOR-
get his offer.

The next day he stopped at our house
to see Eva and to invite us again to go out
on his yacht.

There had once been an article in the
Star about Dr. "Skipper" Fairclough and his
boat. The *Oiseau de la Mer,* moored at the
Windsor Yacht Club, was thirty feet long
with a sleep-in cabin and its own bathroom. Dr. Fairclough had been sailing since
he was a boy but now preferred his motor-
powered yacht.

Eva said to him, "That would be delightful, Doctor. Thank you for inviting
Adele and the boys, too."

My mother declined. "I get seasick on boats. But the boys will love it, I'm sure."

"I will pick you up tomorrow morning."

The next morning my mother packed a picnic basket with sandwiches and cookies she had baked.

While we were waiting, Dr. Fairclough called to say he had an emergency at Hôtel Dieu but would be finished by early afternoon.

He asked my mother if she would bring us to the yacht club at about two. He would meet us there instead. It would save time.

When we arrived at the marina the sky was overcast and there were small whitecaps on the water.

At first I did not recognize Dr. Fairclough when he greeted us. He wore a striped sailor's tee shirt, white pants, and a blue-and-white sailor's cap. He wore loafers without socks.

"Don't worry, it's going to clear up!" Dr. Fairclough said. "All aboard!"

Dr. Fairclough was right, the sun soon came out and the sky turned blue. We cruised along the Detroit River out to Lake St. Clair.

Eva said, "Joseph, Asa, isn't it nice to be on such a marvelous boat? It reminds me of the time I sailed on the China Sea."

"You sailed on the China Sea?" Dr. Fairclough asked. "I've always wanted to do something exotic."

"Well, it wasn't the easiest journey, we had very rough seas, but it was very exciting." Eva smiled at Dr. Fairclough.

"All this fresh air must be very invigorating for you. Do you get to sail often?"

"Not enough. If I had my way I would spend all my time on the water. If one wanted one could go to the Atlantic Ocean from here. I would love to do that one day. Maybe go all the way to Bermuda!"

Eva closed her eyes. "Yes, what a wonderful notion. Sometimes I dream of sailing endlessly around the entire world. Everything is so difficult on land, don't you think, Doctor? There are so many countries and borders and limitations. Sometimes I feel so closed in."

I was surprised she said this since she had told us she was happy living with us in Windsor and that finally, after all her wanderings, she had found a new home.

Why did she say things were so difficult on land? We lived on land. Why did she feel so closed in? She had the nicest room in our house, a room that overlooked the garden.

Dr. Fairclough said, "Well, if you ever wanted I would take you anywhere! Just say the word. Here on the water one can be absolutely free and all those imaginary borders disappear."

"Yes, I suppose they do. It is a wonderful feeling when they do."

She then seemed to remember that Asa and I were there listening.

"Well, I'm just talking nonsense. I would never want to leave my friends."

Dr. Fairclough turned to us. "Are you boys enjoying yourselves?"

"Yes, Dr. Fairclough," Asa said. "It's almost as good as being on an ocean liner!"

W E C R U I S E D for a few hours along the perimeter of the lake. We saw the little cottages on the Canadian shoreline with their weeping willows and pines. Dr. Fairclough then took us along the American shore to see the mansions of Grosse Pointe.

Finally we went farther out into the lake and set anchor.

Eva opened the picnic basket and handed out the sandwiches my mother had prepared. When we finished eating it was already twilight. Dr. Fairclough pulled in the anchor and tried to start up the motor.

The motor would not start. We had run out of gas.

"I can't believe it," Dr. Fairclough said. "I never did that before. I guess I was rushing so much. But don't worry, someone will be by eventually. Just enjoy the water and sky! Actually, this is wonderful. No one can reach me here. I'm free!"

Eva laughed, "Well then, Doctor, I think you may have planned this on purpose."

We floated in the water for an hour or so. Dr. Fairclough showed Asa and me his compass and how to produce the SOS signal on his special light.

Asa began to complain because he could not see well as it grew darker.

"I'm sorry," Dr. Fairclough said. "This might help." He turned a knob and all the lamps on deck lit up.

I was surprised at the remarkable difference these lamps made.

The whole lake seemed to light up.

"Look! Look!"

Eva was pointing to the northern sky over Michigan.

We all turned. To our amazement a great green and red curtain of light shimmered over the horizon.

I had never seen anything like it. It was so brilliant that even Asa was able to see it.

"It's an aurora!" Dr. Fairclough said. "It's an aurora! Why, I have never seen one at this latitude."

"I saw one when I was traveling in Siberia," Eva said. "Do you see it, Asa?"

"Yes, I can see it, Eva." He spoke in awe. "It's so beautiful, Eva."

"Yes, Asa, it is."

When I think back to that moment I am filled with a great sadness. Asa can no longer see such a phenomenon.

Dr. Fairclough laughed and gently hugged Eva around the shoulders with one arm. "Interesting things certainly do happen when the Lady from the East is around."

"It is just a coincidence," Eva said, and the aurora began to fade.

Although I had enjoyed the outing and had been delighted by the aurora, I was suddenly overtaken with nervousness. I had not practiced all afternoon and had not brought my *tiykun* with me. The whole evening would be wasted, too.

I was bound to make a mistake soon if I didn't stop being so careless.

Finally a boat with an American flag approached us and gave us gasoline. The motor started immediately.

A short while later we arrived at the Windsor Yacht Club.

When we got to our house Asa told my mother, "We saw an aurora! We saw an aurora on the lake! Maybe another comet crashed into the sun and the light is changing back!"

CHAPTER 25

I T IS ABOUT A TWENTY-MINUTE walk from the Institute of Anatomy on U Nemocnice to the various buildings of the State Jewish Museum in the Josefov quarter.

After the revolution in 1989, I was invited by the university as a visiting distinguished professor. I was pleased that at this late date there was still a strong interest in my earlier work on the hippocampus and its fiber projections.

Over the last decades the interest in neuroscience had moved on to newer, more sophisticated techniques, in an attempt to answer questions regarding the chemical messengers of the brain, the neurotransmitters, and how to identify and trace their various pathways.

Though there are still many scientists at work using the more old-fashioned approaches, I had noticed a lessening of interest in these older techniques of anatomic investigation. I was beginning to feel a bit like a dinosaur in my laboratory, out of synchrony with the accelerating and highly evolved modern world, stuck in a more comfortable past. Despite all my hard work and success, I did not feel I had accomplished much at all. But in Prague I felt excited about my work again and what I had done with my life. Over the course of eight weeks, I gave a series of lectures and laboratory demonstrations, all of which were enthusiastically attended by faculty and students from various departments, from neurosurgery, neuroscience, and neurology.

As usual Asa had come with me, but most of the time he was not feeling well. He was having one of his recent bouts of depression. These had become more and more frequent after he had become completely blind. The year before our visit to Prague, he lost the last remnant of the tunnel vision through which for decades he had looked out at the world.

Asa spent his days in the apartment that we were given by the university.

"Where are you going?" he would say when he heard me getting ready for one of my walks.

I would tell him that I planned to investigate this or that neighborhood of the city.

"Are you looking for her?"

"For whom?"

"For Eva. Are you still looking for her? Why do you live in the past? Even if she were still alive and living in this city, do you think you could recognize her?"

"I am simply going for a walk, Asa. I have a free day. Do you want to come with me?"

"No thank you, Joseph."

"What will you do with yourself?"

"Think."

"About what?"

"Father and Mother."

"And that's not living in the past?"

"I don't know. Somehow I feel they are with me, part of me somehow, if only I think about them."

I raised my eyebrows, but of course Asa could not see me.

In the evenings, when I was not invited by someone on the university faculty, I would insist that my brother come out with me to dinner. "You cannot stay indoors the whole time. This is getting ridiculous. Will you come with me, Asa?"

He would not answer.

I realized how different we were now. When we were young he would plead with me until I said what he wanted to hear. Now I couldn't help but repeat myself. I heard the pleading tone in my own voice, which was disorienting to me. I felt slightly dizzy.

"Will you come with me, Asa?"

In the end Asa would be obedient and get dressed. He would even put on a tie and sport jacket. Oddly, despite himself, he seemed to enjoy these evening excursions to a restaurant. When we were on the street a smile would hover on his face.

On one occasion he stopped and turned to me:

"Do you remember when Father drew pictures for us?"

I didn't.

"Yes, he used to draw us alligators and crocodiles and ask us what the difference was."

"I forgot all about that. Yes, I do remember now. I'm surprised you remember it. You were so little then."

"I remember lots of things, Joseph. Why are you always so surprised? I just remembered something else."

"What?"

"I'll show you in the restaurant."

Sitting at the restaurant table, Asa asked me for a piece of paper and a pen. I placed the pen in his hand and guided it to the piece of paper. Despite his blindness he drew precisely. He combined the symbol of a tree with the symbol of the sun coming up behind it, the pictogram for east— Higashi.

Asa laughed. "See, I do remember lots of things, Joseph. I've stored things up for the lean years."

"Yes, I suppose you have." I hesitated, then said, "You know, Asa, I'm sorry your vision is all gone now. I really am. It saddens me, too."

"I know, Joseph." Asa smiled. "I just remembered something else, something Eva said when she first came to us." He spoke slowly, almost in a whisper. " 'We all own something more important, our souls, which are more important than our human bodies and our senses. No one can ever take your soul away from you. Your soul is forever.'—Do you remember, Joseph?"

"Yes."

Asa said, "You see, Joseph. You and I are different even if we both remember the same things after all these years. You cling too much to your memories, as if they were . . . well, as if they were objects you could forever hold in your hands. But they are not. I have tried to learn from my memories. That's what's important to me. Things have always been difficult for me and there are times when it all seems too much, but I am still better off because of what I heard from a stranger who once came to our house. But that was long ago, Joseph, and far away."

As we walked home from the restaurant, Asa slipped back into his quiet mood.

I found myself staring at my brother.

I was overcome by my old foolish thoughts, which once formed in youth are so hard to erase.

Asa is still beautiful, I found myself saying to myself, and he is paying for it with his bouts of depression. After all these years I was alarmed to find myself repeating the childish things I had told myself when I was a boy:

Because I was ugly I would somehow be safe from some of the terrible things that happened to other people.

I would not go blind like my brother, Asa, or wither and turn yellow like my father.

I would be happy someday, even if I was not happy then!

DURING MY FREE TIME, and I had a great deal over those eight weeks, I spent many afternoons walking through the city. It was just as well that Asa would not join me for these excursions. There were things I wanted to do alone.

The first time I visited the Hradčany Castle I was saddened. Despite its splendor it was not at all like the fantasy castle I conjured up so vividly at Eva's command all those years ago when we took her to see the countryside around Windsor.

I found myself returning over and over to the various buildings that constituted the Jewish Museum. After the Second World War the museum was taken over by the Czechoslovakian state at the request of the remnant Jewish community, which did not have the strength or resources to look after it on its own.

I made inquiries and became acquainted with several members of the staff. There were no longer any survivors from the terrible period of the war who were still working. Most of the current curators were born after the war.

No one had known Enoch Laquedem personally. His name was only vaguely familiar to a few.

Someone, however, told me about an old woman who had been conscripted as a sorter of textiles in the museum during the war. She had eventually been deported like all of those who had worked in the museum. Somehow she managed to survive. She lived in the Letná district north across the Vltava.

A meeting was arranged.

The small house on a tiny side street was covered in vines. It was very dark inside.

The old woman spoke Czech and German, the latter I had learned as an adult, mainly to read scientific sources in the original. More than once Dr. Schpizhof said to me, "If a parrot with its small mantle of neural tissue can understand English, you can learn German. You have a bigger brain. Besides, it is important that you be able to read the early anatomic literature."

Dr. Schpizhof's words led me not only to the study of German but to a period in which I worked on the pallium of birds, the smooth, gray-white covering of avian brain, the equivalent of our human and mammalian cerebral hemispheres. I published five papers on the subject.

The old woman in Letná had not known Laquedem very well.

"He was a quiet man," she said. "We never actually spoke to one another, though he always nodded in a friendly way when no one was looking. It was a small gesture but it made me feel I was still alive. I was so dead inside."

She had not remembered anything about books or manuscripts that came to the museum during that time.

The old woman in Letná had little formal education. She had been brought to the museum in 1943. The original experts on textiles had already been taken by the earlier transports. She had worked once at a mill, that was her only prior experience, and had been brought to the museum by the Germans to sort valuable textiles that were still coming in from the surrounding communities. These were mostly the gold and silver embroidered Torah mantles, and the elaborate *parochos*—curtains that hung at the front of the Holy Arks, which were confiscated from synagogues before the buildings were destroyed.

The old woman did not know anything about manuscripts in the museum nor had she heard of the *Augsburg Miscellany.*

She did remember that the museum was forced to mount various exhibits for high officials of the Nazi party. "Many of us prisoners took our job of preservation very seriously," she said proudly. "We hoped we could at least save many of our people's treasures. There were catalogues, too, for each exhibit."

"Catalogues?"

"Yes, there were several exhibits mounted for the party dignitaries."

With that information I returned to the museum. In its archives I was led to the single copy of the exhibit catalogue entitled "Books and Manuscripts of the Jews." Among others was a description of a lavishly illuminated holiday prayer book illustrated by Alexander of Augsburg, the *De Braga Maḥzor.*

I read this account in a sort of shock. I asked the curator to see the manuscript. He looked at the old catalogue. He seemed puzzled but promised to look through the extensive museum inventory. His search lasted almost two weeks.

"I cannot find it," the curator finally told me, shrugging his shoulders. "It must have disappeared during the war. Lots of things disappeared, you understand. I do not know what became of it. It is very discouraging to think about, Professor."

I finally told the curator that in my youth I had seen the other example of the work of Alexander of Augsburg, the *Augsburg Miscellany*.

This excited the curator so much that he showed me other catalogues from other exhibits and even some of the guest books signed by the high dignitaries who came to see the exhibit of the soon-to-be extinct race.

I glanced at the guest book without much interest, but my eye caught one name, a visitor of high party rank. He signed his name in an old-fashioned educated handwriting:

Dr. Xavier I. Hirschmann, *Professor für Nahöstliche Wissenschaft und Semitische Sprachen*—Professor of Near-East Studies and Semitic Languages—*Universität Berlin*.

CHAPTER 26

HANKS TO ISABEL KREMLACH'S
efforts, my mother was hired to cater the
Mizrachi Women's annual summer luncheon. This event was always held in July on
the shores of Lake St. Claire, where many
Windsor people had summer cottages.

A catered affair was an innovation for
the group. In the past all the membership
women brought simple cold dairy foods
with them. But this year Isabel Kremlach
was the new president of the Mizrachi
Women's chapter, and she insisted on
changes at the planning meeting, especially since the luncheon was to be held at
her cottage.

"Really, ladies, it would be more elegant if we had it catered. It will draw more people, we can charge more, and we will raise more money. Spend a little more, make a little more! National headquarters will be very happy with us. Our chapter will certainly get the Tree of Life Certificate.

"Now that we have a real cateress in town it would be easy. Adele is not expensive. And I'm so tired of cottage cheese and cling peaches! *¡Dios mío!* My poor colon! It rebels against such insults! In Havana such things would be unheard of!"

"This is not Havana, Isabel!" someone shouted.

"That is the tragedy of my life!" Isabel rolled her eyes in mock despair. "As I always say, *todo por el amor!*"

All the women laughed.

Isabel surveyed the room. "So I say, ladies, the matter is settled. Adele has agreed to make pastries, sandwiches, and blintzes. Perfect for a summer afternoon. Now let's vote with a show of hands. Come, raise those hands. You there. *¡Vaga!* Raise that lazy hand!"

"You know very well I broke my collarbone, Isabel."

"That's why God gave you two hands, Sarah."

ISABEL KREMLACH was right. The catered affair drew more people. Nearly fifty women responded. There might be even more coming, "what with the stragglers and *neet*-wits," Isabel said.

My mother was nervous as this was only her second big

event, after the Zubrovskys' wedding. Although everyone was happy with the Zubrovsky affair, and many people had told her how delicious the food was, even Iris May, this did not make my mother feel any more secure.

"There are so many people coming and everything has to be perfect, Joseph. I'll need all the help I can get so you will have to look after Asa."

"I have to practice."

"Yes, I know, but you can keep an eye on your brother from time to time."

She turned to Eva. "I hope I can do this. I don't know why I'm so nervous. The girls who worked for me at the Zubrovsky wedding are away in Nova Scotia."

"Don't worry, Adele, I will help you," Eva promised. "It will be a big success."

"But you have to work on your father's book."

"I can still take time off to help you."

The entire week before the luncheon, my mother was busy shopping for various ingredients.

Two days before the luncheon my mother got up early to bake the pastries. Even though the women ordered and paid for only two kinds my mother wanted to make three varieties. After much consideration, she decided on custard-filled Ladies-in-Waiting, cherry-centered Robin Red Breasts, and chocolate-covered Paradise Wheels.

Whenever I needed a break from practicing, I would come in and watch what was going on.

Eva came downstairs to help my mother.

"Forgive me, Adele. I must have overslept. I was up late reading again that article you found for me last week."

"That's all right, Eva. You're just in time. I'm ready to put the cherries in the Robin Red Breasts."

Even though she had come to help in the kitchen, Eva was all dressed up in a yellow silk dress.

"Eva, you should change first. You'll ruin your clothes!"

"Oh, I will be fine. I'll put on one of your aprons."

Eva was right. She did not get any stains on her clothes.

Asa was outside wearing the silk veiling. We watched him through the kitchen windows and open back door, running around the sundial and between the rows of flowers.

Asa was playing a new game he had invented since Eva came, Emperor's Zoo. He was the Great Khan and went around taking care of all the exotic animals in his menagerie, which lived secretly in our backyard. It was a full-time job. Every day new creatures arrived by ship from various parts of the world. LaLa GooGoo, the green horse who could climb and hide high in the trees like a chameleon. You always had to look up when you walked in the garden in case LaLa GooGoo was sitting above you and was "going to the bathroom." And there was Abulabaz, the magic elephant raised in the jungle by nightingales. Abulabaz had learned a new trick. He could disguise himself as a rose. No one would notice this until they tried to pluck the rose or move it, since it was as heavy as the elephant itself. Also, despite its appearance, the rose smelled like an elephant. Still, Asa explained, it was a remarkable feat to look like a rose.

"Eva, Eva," Asa called out from the garden. "Look!" He pretended he could not with all his strength budge the crimson flower on one of the rosebushes. "It's Abulabaz, the emperor's elephant!"

Eva wiped her hands on her apron.

"I'll come out and look. But only for a minute, since I must help your mother. She has so much work!"

Eva went out the back door into the garden. I watched her with Asa as she pretended to struggle to move the rose, which was really Abulabaz.

Just then the doorbell rang.

Isabel Kremlach had called the *Star* and suggested that Geneviève LaFontaine interview my mother. "Publicity, Adele, that's what you need to build up your business. People have to start thinking, kosher cateress, kosher cateress. And it will be good for our Mizrachi membership, too."

Geneviève LaFontaine had arrived on her bicycle. She had leaned it on one of the large rosebushes out front, tearing off several flowers in the process.

"Your baking smells divine," she told my mother as she made her way through our house to the kitchen.

She looked at me, then turned quickly to my mother. "It's so nice your boy is helping you. My son won't go near the kitchen. He's just like his father. They are both allergic to women's work! Men! Can't cook with them. No use cooking without them!

"May I sit here?"

Before my mother could answer, Geneviève LaFontaine

sat down on one of the kitchen seats and took out a stenographer's notebook. She wrote in shorthand as my mother explained her various recipes.

"Uh-huh . . . I see . . . Are there any special ingredients you use? Forgive me, I'm so ignorant about your people's customs. I know you wouldn't use lard or anything like that." She giggled. "Your people are dead set against the poor little pig. Am I right?"

My mother nodded.

"Do you ever use butter?"

My mother smiled. "Yes. Whenever I can. The Mizrachi luncheon will be a dairy meal. The main course is blintzes, they're like crêpes filled with cheese or fruit. I'll make them the day of the luncheon. Today I'm making the pastries. But I don't use butter if I am going to serve dessert after a meat meal. We don't mix dairy and meat."

Geneviève LaFontaine burst into laughter and loudly clapped her hands as if she had heard the funniest joke. "Yes, yes, I remember, your mixing rule! That's an old rule worth keeping, I should say." She leaned forward in her seat and waved her index finger. "It's not good to mix things too much!" Geneviève LaFontaine laughed again. "Your people have a good point there! Look at me. I'm practically a mongrel myself." She began counting on her long bony fingers. "Let's see. I have French and Scottish and English and even a drop of Italian blood in me. And God only knows what—"

The sky outside brightened. Something shifted into sunlight. Eva had come back into the kitchen from the backyard. Even though she was wearing a plain apron she appeared luminous, her hair lit up from the light streaming in from the back door.

Geneviève LaFontaine brought her bony hand to her chest.

"Well, I'll be! I've seen you before! I know I have. Yes. On Ouellette. I'll never forget that. You said you were just visiting our pretty little town. I have been hoping I would find you again! I thought, maybe I was dreaming. You were wearing the most wonderful blue. I never can get away with colors like that." She pulled at her white blouse, which looked worn and faded. "I make all my clothes myself and it shows! Well, we usually don't have so much glamour in our city. But you, you are so . . . so soignée.

"Who are you? What are you doing here?"

"I am renting a room."

Geneviève LaFontaine spread out her arms. "A duchess renting a room! A queen in the dungeon! Marvelous! And it must be confusing for you with all these curious customs."

"I am quite familiar with them."

"Really?" Geneviève said.

Eva smiled but it was not her usual smile.

"Well, you must forgive me," Geneviève began again. "I'm cross-examining you as if you were under arrest! Now please tell me all about yourself. Let me guess. You're from New York City or Paris. I've never been in either place but one day I will. I've been writing for the *Star* for ten years and I guess I'm just a hopeless people person. People are my specialty. Even as a little girl, my mother would say to me, 'Geneviève Orestes'—that's my maiden name, as I've said

I'm quite a mishmash—'Geneviève Orestes, you never do stop asking personal questions! One day you will get into big trouble!'"

"I do have a terrible headache," Eva said. "Please forgive me. I'm not used to this heat. I need to lie down. I know Adele has so much to tell you about the upcoming luncheon."

Geneviève waved her finger at Eva and laughed. "My lovely, you can't get away that easy! I'll come back for you, now that I know where to find you!"

Eva smiled, turned, and left the kitchen.

Geneviève called after Eva. "I promise I won't hurt you! I will only adore you!"

Geneviève then asked my mother, "Who is she?"

"Now, Mrs. LaFontaine, everyone is entitled to their privacy, don't you think?"

"Of course, of course, I meant no harm."

Geneviève then looked out the back door and saw Asa moving through the garden. In all this time she had not noticed him.

"Oh, I thought I saw a garden fairy! There's a little boy with drapery over his head."

"That's my son Asa. He just covers his head to protect his eyes from the sun. They are a little weak."

Geneviève said, "Oh, yes. I need new glasses myself. My husband keeps saying, 'Genevièvey, you are practically glued to the page! Pull back, pull back, would you?'"

Geneviève LaFontaine became quiet a moment, staring out the back door. She turned to face my mother.

"Is it all right if I peek at your garden? It looks so lovely."

"Yes, of course, I'll show you."

"No, no. You have so much work to do. I'll go out myself. Just for a moment. I'm not fragile. I'll just take a peek. I love flowers."

She went outside and walked through the yard. She approached Asa and asked him something. He walked around with her pointing to various bushes. He pointed upward to the trees. Geneviève LaFontaine giggled.

They stopped and talked a few moments.

When Geneviève LaFontaine returned to the kitchen she said to my mother, "I couldn't tell at first, what with his veil, but your boy is cute as a button. And he has such a lively imagination! Singing elephants and green horses and such!"

The next day there was a story in the *Star*, in Geneviève LaFontaine's popular weekly column, "N'est-ce pas?":

Every day we encounter people to whom we never give a second thought. But one early morning, quite by chance, I saw a remarkable creature looking dreamily into Lazare's Furs even though it was such warm weather. She carried the most brilliant parasol. It was a sunny day. She stood there, so statuesque and regal, one foot turned out ever so slightly. Of course, I went right over to her and asked if she was new in Windsor. All she said was, "I'm just visiting for a few hours. What a pretty town you have." I never thought we would cross paths again. I never dreamed of such a story filled with so much romance and tragicalness!

Just yesterday I discovered the mysterious and beautiful lady I had seen that day just a few weeks ago. But she was as discreet as an aristocrat so I had to go to my secret sources. Of course, I cannot reveal her name. Everyone is entitled to their privacy. What I can tell you is this: She has traveled the world and even lived in Japan for ten years with her late Japanese husband. He was a famous doctor who cared for the emperor! Our mystery lady certainly has moved in the highest society. And my sources tell me she has a remarkable treasure worth a small fortune. I do not know yet what it is. She carries it with her all the time. Imagine such goings on here in Windsor.

A much smaller article appeared on the opposite page:

LADIES OF THE MOSAIC FAITH TO HOLD GALA LUNCHEON

The local chapter of Mizrachi Ladies, a Zionist organization, is holding what promises to be a delightful affair to raise money for their unfortunate co-religionists in the former Palestine. The mise-en-scène is the lakefront cottage of Mrs. Isabel Kremlach, wife of Rabbi Maurice Kremlach of the Shaarei Chesed Synagogue. The cateress for the event is Adele Ivri. Mrs. Ivri, a widow, is a soft-spoken and homey woman with simple yet firmly held beliefs.

Havana-born Isabel Kremlach, luncheon hostess

and president of the local chapter, said, "Oh, Adele is the best thing that's happened to our community in a long while. We are so happy to have our own cateress to meet our unique needs. Of course, all denominations are welcome to join us for this happy event."

Underneath was a recipe: Adele Ivri's Dairy Paradise Wheels.

My mother turned pale when she saw the article about Eva. "This is terrible," she said to me, "we promised her. This is terrible. Eva will be so upset."

"Asa's such a blabbermouth. It's his fault."

"He's just a child," my mother said. "Mrs. LaFontaine had no business asking him nosy questions. I better go tell Eva."

I followed my mother upstairs.

"I'm so sorry," my mother said, handing Eva the newspaper. "Please forgive us. I hope you won't be angry."

We watched nervously while Eva read the article.

Finally Eva said, "Don't worry. I'm not upset or angry. It does not mention my name, or what the treasure is. It doesn't matter anyway. I always keep the miscellany in sight. I will just have to be extra careful."

My mother was so relieved by Eva's reaction that she had tears in her eyes.

I remained nervous. I did not believe Eva. I could not believe she was not upset. How could she not be angry with us? How could she feel safe living in our house? I did not know what to do. Asa had ruined everything.

That night I could not sleep from worry. What if someone tried to break into our house and steal Eva's treasure?

Now I would have to practice the *parsha* even harder.

AT THE MIZRACHI LUNCHEON the women gathered around Eva. Everyone clearly knew that she was the mystery woman that Geneviève LaFontaine had written about.

"Is it true you have a treasure?" someone asked.

Eva laughed. "Well, I did buy this when I came to your lovely town." She held up her arm. The ruby bracelet from Shooshy Kalkstein's estate sparkled in the afternoon light. "I didn't know it was that valuable. Tomorrow I will put it in a safety box at the bank!"

All the women laughed.

Someone else asked, "Was your husband really the physician to the emperor of Japan?"

"No," Eva said. "I do not know where she got that. Though my husband was from an aristocratic family."

She then told everyone how her husband had saved her life by getting her out of Prague, and how the Japanese were so kind to her.

"Oh, but weren't you afraid!" one of the ladies asked. "All those atomic bombs!"

Eva looked suddenly sad.

"No, no. I was never afraid. But my husband was in the prefecture that day working at the children's hospital. He was exposed to the radiation. He became very sick and died." She paused a moment. "My husband was a wonderful man. He always knew my heart."

A hush spread through the crowd. The women were teary-eyed.

Eva said, "You are all very kind to listen to me. Please forgive me. I didn't mean to talk of such things. I suppose it's time to taste all the delicious treats Adele has made."

EARLY THAT EVENING, after they had returned from the luncheon, Eva went to pay my mother for that week's room and board.

"Oh, no, Eva," my mother said. "I couldn't take money from you this week. You helped me so much with the luncheon."

"I was happy to, Adele. You are so generous to me. If you're not too tired we can go over the last article you found for me at the library. I read it a third time last night. It's astonishing how close Ugaritic is to Hebrew. The tablets they found in Syria are astounding. They shed so much light on everything. They confirm many of the things my father wrote. Why don't we talk about it tonight if you're not tired. I know you've had such a busy day and week. We can sit in the garden around the sundial."

"I would love that, Eva."

"I'm glad. I want to read you the introduction of my father's book. I think you can help me answer a question that has been bothering me there."

"Me? I'm just the student. I'm not sure I will have anything intelligent to say."

"But you always do, Adele. You always do."

C H A P T E R   2 7

HE DOORBELL RANG.

Eva was coming down the stairs. "Who is it, Adele?"

"There's a telegram for you."

"For me?" Eva went over and took the telegram from the delivery man. He blushed when she thanked him.

She opened the envelope. She appeared annoyed.

My mother asked, "What is it, Eva?"

"Would you like to see it?" She handed my mother the telegram.

```
Dear Miss Laquedem:
    It is the daunting task of
the Commission on European
```

Jewish Cultural Reconstruction to find various objects important to the Jewish heritage
and unaccounted for at the close of war. Our
director, Dr. Hannah Arendt, has been traveling through the Mid-West and is currently
in Detroit. She has just discovered that you
are in nearby Windsor, Canada. She would be
extremely grateful to you for any assistance
you may be able to give us in this sacred
endeavor. The director would like to meet
with you as soon as possible as her schedule
is heavy and she must leave for Europe
very soon.

At the end of the telegram was a number in Detroit where the director was staying.

My mother said, "It sounds important, Eva. Will you be able to help them?"

"I don't know. How could I? So much is always expected of me." She paused a moment. "Yes, I will try and help. Would you mind very much calling them for me, Adele? They may come tomorrow morning if they want."

"Of course, I don't mind at all."

"You are good to me, Adele. I hope you will forgive me for taking your time. I must get back to work. It is such a re-sponsibility. Sometimes I feel overwhelmed. There is yet an-other article I will have to ask you to find in Detroit, on literary forms in the Ugaritic myths. It is a shame I am un-able to go myself. I'm sorry to trouble you so much."

"It's no problem, Eva. I love finding things for you. I always learn something."

THE NEXT MORNING, a Friday, my mother drove across the border to the library at Wayne State University and searched for the journal article that Eva needed. They did not carry it at Assumption College in Windsor.

"I'm sorry to trouble you so much," Eva repeated as my mother was leaving the house. "Especially today."

"I'm happy to do it, Eva. It's so exciting for me. I can be back in two or three hours. These summer days are so long and there will be plenty of time to prepare for Shabbes."

Asa went along for the ride.

A short while after they left, a Detroit taxi drove up to our house. A woman got out. She had dark black hair and wore a gray skirt and frilly white blouse. She walked up the pathway between the roses.

I greeted her at the door.

The woman smiled and asked my name.

"Joseph is an excellent name. My name is Hannah Arendt. I've come to see Miss Laquedem."

I went upstairs to get Eva. When she came out of the room she whispered softly, "Would you stay with me and help me should I need anything for the visitor? You were so helpful to me, Joseph, when the emissaries came from Jerusalem."

I did not know how I had helped her with the emissaries, but I understood that for some reason she did not want to be alone with her visitor; that had been the case as well when the emissaries came.

It pleased me to think that somehow I could make Eva feel comfortable and calm. I was like the bodyguard or the chamberlain to the queen. Although a queen might be the most powerful person in the land, she still needed her guards and advisors to support her. How else could she take care of so many things? I was proud that Eva wanted me to stay with her, and was happy she had sent my mother and Asa on a long errand.

In the living room, the visitor greeted Eva in German.

Eva shook her hand and answered in English. "Why don't we sit here in the living room?"

Dr. Arendt nodded at me.

"Joseph will be joining us," Eva said.

"Well, if you wish," she said doubtfully.

Dr. Arendt sat on the wing chair. I sat next to Eva on the sofa, just as I had when the emissaries came. At first Eva did not take my hand.

I was proud of Eva. She was so beautiful. All sorts of important people came to see her.

Sitting across from Eva, the visitor seemed so homely.

She said, "Years ago, when I was a student in Heidelberg, I heard your father lecture on the subject of prophecy. I was in the philosophy department then, completing my dissertation on the concept of love in Saint Augustine. Your father's notion of the *Netz der Wirklichkeit*—the net of reality— made a strong impression on me. I was quite taken with his ideas. In some ways, of course, the concept seems obvious, and yet your father explained it in the most original and interesting manner. Nowadays I find those unexpected connections everywhere I go."

Eva smiled. "Yes, these connections are always taking us by surprise, but in truth they are the natural order of things."

"They can be very unsettling, too, don't you think?" Dr. Arendt paused a moment and stared at Eva.

Eva took my hand. Her hand was cold.

Dr. Arendt continued.

"Speaking of the net of reality, I suppose you are wondering how I found you. Much to my surprise I learned from Professor Xavier Hirschmann that the daughter of Enoch Laquedem had been in the area. But Hirschmann would not say where you went. I did not expect I would find you so easily. I heard of your whereabouts quite by chance through the Amitzer Rebbe.

"I thought it odd that you met with Professor Hirschmann, though I suppose you could think the same of me."

"Why do you say that? He was a colleague of my father."

Dr. Arendt looked at Eva a long time and then at me. She said something in German.

Eva said, "Whatever you have to tell me you can tell me in English."

I had an awful feeling. I began to feel nervous. It occurred to me that Eva had asked me to join her in the living room to bear witness again. I could not imagine for what. What could she want from me? I did not know. Even to this day I do not know why she wanted me there. Perhaps she did not know either. Did she think I could protect her from bad news?

Dr. Arendt said, "If you wish. I do not have time to mince words. Herr Professor Hirschmann has told you of his distinguished academic and clerical background?"

"He has written in many of the same journals as my father. I recently found some of his old articles in the *Biblische Monatsschrift* and—"

Arendt waved her hand. "Yes, he is quite an expert, and a Nazi, too. That is why he was sent in 1942 to Prague."

Eva turned pale. "Prague? He told me he had never been to Prague."

"Professor Hirschmann was sent to Prague to evaluate the manuscripts and books being confiscated from all over Bohemia and Moravia and being sent to the Jewish Museum. When Professor Hirschmann arrived your father was no longer doing his regular work, of course. He was a slave laborer sorting books and manuscripts."

"A 'slave laborer'?" I felt Eva's hand trembling ever so slightly in mine.

Dr. Arendt made a noise like a snort. "You surprise me for such a sophisticated young woman. And a scientist, too."

Eva just looked at her.

Dr. Arendt continued, "Of course, Professor Hirschmann was very interested in your father."

"My father?"

"Yes, yes, your father." She sounded exasperated. "We believe that Hirschmann helped himself to several manuscripts from the museum's original collection and those that arrived from the lootings. It is hard to prove without the right evidence. He has become very wealthy for a refugee cleric."

Eva nodded gravely. "I still do not understand, Frau Professor. Why did he lie to me?"

"The world is filled with liars. You cannot spend your whole life pretending that is not so."

"But then why did you meet with him? And why did he agree to meet with you?"

"Because we can make things unpleasant for him if he does not cooperate. He has many things we want and that were obtained by illegal means. But we must be careful to get them back safely. It is a very delicate and complex situation. We cannot afford to make any foolish mistakes. Mistakes can have severe consequences."

"What does this have to do with me?"

"Did Hirschmann show you anything from his own collection? Did he show you the *De Braga Maḥzor*? During the war it was confiscated in Brno and brought to the Jewish Museum. The original owners are dead. Now it is missing. We believe Professor Hirschmann stole it."

"He did not show me anything but his money. He wanted something from me."

"Yes, he told me. He knew your father owned the *Augsburg Miscellany*. It was no secret. He wanted that, too, for his own collection. Collectors can be quite obsessed. It is that old *cupiditas*—the desire for material things. But the professor had to be extremely careful. He could not be caught taking things that were now the property of the Reich. And he needed help in altering the entries to the vast inventories that were assembled. Still, he was willing to take some risks."

" 'Risks'?"

Dr. Arendt spoke slowly, as if to a child.

"Professor Hirschmann offered your father his life if he would give him the *Augsburg Miscellany*."

" 'His life'?" Eva pulled her hand out of mine. I thought she was going to faint as she had when the emissaries told her that her father had been hanged. Somehow she controlled herself. She sat stiffly on the sofa.

Dr. Arendt continued. "I cannot say if what he says is true or not. Professor Hirschmann claims he had offered to drive your father himself in his own car to Switzerland. The Frau Professor was Swiss. The Hirschmanns drove back and forth all the time with little trouble. Though it would have been dangerous for them if they were caught. But your father did not have what he wanted."

Eva turned ashen. "Of course he didn't. I took it."

"So it appears. But your father would not tell Hirschmann that. He was afraid it might put you in danger, what with the alliance of Germany and Japan. He was not sure you would be out of his reach. He told Professor Hirschmann it had been stolen. Professor Hirschmann did not believe him. He kept your father alive as long as he could, even as other workers in the museum were sent to the transports. He thought your father would eventually agree to give up the manuscript. But it did not take long for Hirschmann to find out that your father had a daughter and that she had left Europe. He put two and two together.

"After that, Hirschmann had no more use for your father." Dr. Arendt paused a moment. "I do not believe the rest of his story."

" 'The rest of his story'?"

Dr. Arendt took in a deep breath. "I do not like being involved in all this unpleasantness. It is too depressing and time-consuming, I have so much of my own work to do."

"Please tell me."

"I assume the daughter of Enoch Laquedem would have responded had Professor Hirschmann tried to reach her in Japan."

Eva looked confused. "What did you say?"

"Did anyone ever try contacting you in Japan?"

Eva spoke in barely a whisper. "No. No one ever tried to reach me there. No one. I heard once from my father a few weeks after I arrived. Perhaps someone tried but I was often traveling with my husband."

"When was your husband executed? My information is not clear on that, 1944? . . . I'm sorry, I cannot hear you."

"No, 1943."

It took me a moment to understand. Eva had lied. Her husband did not die from the atomic bomb.

Why did she lie and say he had died from the atomic bomb?

Why did she say he was sick for several years?

Eva was a liar. The world was filled with liars, and Eva was one of them.

Dr. Arendt said, "I'm sorry about your husband. He tried to help the Chinese, didn't he?"

Eva nodded again.

"The communists?"

"No, no, the nationalists."

"Were you allowed to travel much after that?"

"No," Eva said, "not during the war." She covered her face with her hands.

Dr. Arendt stood up. She went over to Eva. She paused a moment as if deciding what to do. She lifted Eva's head gently in her hands. Eva was crying.

Hannah Arendt bent over and kissed Eva on the forehead as if in reconciliation.

For a long time she stood before Eva.

Finally she said, "I am sorry, Mrs. Higashi. There is one more thing I must ask you. The *Augsburg Miscellany* is a great treasure of our people's culture. So much was destroyed. A museum in Jerusalem is interested in buying it. There it can be studied and seen by many people. They can arrange a fair and generous offer if you are willing to part with it."

Eva could not speak. She waved Dr. Arendt away with her hand.

"Do not decide now. Think about it carefully. There is no rush. It may be a good opportunity for you." She handed Eva a card. "I do not wish to be alarmist. Professor Hirschmann is a weak man, I do not think he can do anything to you. But I do not trust him. I'm afraid it won't take long for him to find out where you are. I'm surprised he hasn't already."

Eva was silent.

Dr. Arendt turned to me. I stood up.

"I am pleased to have met you, Joseph. I wish you good fortune. I know you've heard many terrible things. It is very upsetting, even for adults, but we must be hopeful for the future."

I did not know what to say. I simply nodded.

"I will find my way out. My driver is waiting. Stay with her until she is better."

After Dr. Arendt left, Eva remained sitting on the sofa. I stayed in the living room just as I had been asked to do. Eva did not seem to know I was there.

All these years later I am still ashamed of my reaction at that time. I could not help myself. I was suddenly angry. It was an anger so strong that it both surprised and frightened me.

Eva paid no attention to me. She had asked me to be there with her, she had acted as if we were the same, and then she ignored me. She sat on the sofa staring blankly.

I knew she had just learned something awful, that she had taken the very thing that might have saved her father's life. Her father had forbidden her to take it and she disobeyed and he was killed.

Perhaps that is why she was punished and had to wander the world.

Even then I knew that my thoughts were shameful. It occurred to me that perhaps it would have made no difference had she not taken the *Augsburg Miscellany* with her. Professor Hirschmann would have tricked her father and taken the manuscript. He would not have saved Enoch

Laquedem's life. She had been brave to take the miscellany. I could never be so brave. I could never be like her. How could I have ever thought we were the same?

How could I think of my own feelings at such a time? Still, I was angry.

Sitting there on the sofa, Eva seemed more beautiful than the first time I saw her. Her red hair had loosened ever so slightly and seemed more abundant and luxurious than before. The skin on her hands and legs was smooth and pale. And because she was so beautiful she seemed to be moving farther away from me and the small world I knew.

I realized then that she would leave us. She would leave us as my father had left us, and as she had left her own father. She had already forgotten me.

I kept thinking, She asked me to stay with her and now she has forgotten me, though I am standing here before her. She is going to leave.

I began to panic.

A HALF HOUR LATER my mother came home with Asa. Eva was still sitting on the living room sofa, staring in front of her.

My mother came into the room all excited. "Eva, guess what? I found the article you wanted and another one that is so interesting I couldn't help reading it right there in the—

"What's the matter, Eva?"

Eva looked up.

"I'm fine, Adele. Would you mind calling Dr. Fairclough for me?"

"Eva, what's wrong?"

Eva got up slowly and went to the stairs. She finally turned to my mother. She smoothed her hair with her hands. "I'll be fine, Adele. I just need to rest a bit. But I'd be grateful if Dr. Fairclough would come see me as soon as possible."

As Eva went upstairs, my mother asked me urgently, "What happened, Joseph?"

"I don't know," I lied. "The lady from that commission came. They talked a long time. I didn't understand anything. They spoke in another language."

CHAPTER 28

HAT AFTERNOON, DR. FAIR-
clough came to see Eva. He went upstairs
and spoke with her privately in her room.

Eva reminded him of the promise he
made the day we went out on the lake and
saw the aurora:

"If you ever wanted I would take you
anywhere! Here on the water one can be absolutely free and all the borders disappear."

"I WILL LEAVE TOMORROW," she
told my mother after Dr. Fairclough left
the house. Dr. Fairclough had agreed to
come in the morning and take Eva away on
the *Oiseau de la Mer.*

"But why?" my mother said.

"I have found out that Professor Hirschmann is an evil man. He may try to find me here."

"But we can tell the police. They'll protect you. How can he hurt you?"

Eva smiled as if talking to a child. "No, Adele. That would not do."

"Eva, please don't go. You cannot always be running away. That never solves anything."

"Sometimes it is all one can do, Adele."

"Sometimes, but not anymore. You're upset, Eva. Please wait. Please stay a while longer, then decide."

"I can't, Adele. I'm sorry."

"But where will things be different? Where will things be better?"

Eva smiled. "I've been meaning to give you this, Adele." She removed the ruby bracelet that she had bought the day she arrived in Windsor. She pressed it in my mother's hands.

"No, I cannot accept such a valuable thing," my mother said and gave it back to Eva.

Eva continued to insist but my mother remained firm. "No, no, Eva. I cannot accept it. You may need it one day. It must be worth a small fortune."

THAT EVENING after the Sabbath began, Eva did not join us for dinner. She stayed in her room and packed her trunk.

Except for the blessings, we ate our Sabbath meal in silence. Afterward I went out into the garden and watched Eva through the windows. She moved back and forth through her lighted room, just as she had the evening she arrived, holding in her hands objects that I could not quite make out, undulating forms that projected with her shadow on the curtains.

THAT NIGHT I dreamed that Eva and my father were walking through our garden looking at the roses I had planted.

"What gorgeous flowers Joseph has planted!" they exclaimed. "Yes, yes. Look how they've grown!"

My father smiled at Eva and asked her, "What are these flowers called?"

"Why, they're Evening Faces, Mr. Ivri," Eva said, and suddenly she began to turn pale and yellow like my father.

I was so startled I awoke in a sweat and could not sleep the rest of the night.

SHORTLY AFTER DAWN I heard Dr. Fairclough arrive in his station wagon.

I got out of bed and dressed. I passed by Eva's door. It was open.

Eva was standing near the bed with Dr. Fairclough. She was wearing the same shimmering blue-green dress that she had worn the day she came to live with us.

I realized the room had changed back again to what it

was before she arrived, only now it seemed to me even more dull and colorless, despite the sunlight streaming inside.

All her beautiful things had been packed.

"Good morning, Joseph," she said. "Do you think you could help the doctor with my trunk? I'm sorry to trouble you."

Although it was the Sabbath, I helped Dr. Fairclough carry Eva's trunk downstairs and out to the car.

"You are getting very strong!" Dr. Fairclough said, out of breath.

After we finished putting the trunk in the car, Dr. Fairclough came back to the house to get Eva.

She came down the stairs. She put down her handbag on the bottom of the stairway. Just as when she arrived, it contained her two most important treasures, the manuscript of *Clouds of Glory*, and the *Augsburg Miscellany*.

I could see a corner of the lacquerware box that held the miscellany peeking out from the top. I thought of Mrs. Miyashita and wondered if she ever found her daughter, and if so did her daughter love her again.

Eva turned and smiled at Dr. Fairclough. "I am very grateful to you, Doctor. I don't know what I would do without your help."

"I'm glad to be of help, though I will be sad to see you go."

Eva said, "I would like a few minutes with my friends, Doctor. Would you excuse me?"

"Of course, Madame. We have all the time in the world." He bowed. "The captain is at your service."

Dr. Fairclough went out to wait on the front porch.

Eva came into the living room. My mother and Asa had just come downstairs. Eva stood a little distance from us. It was as if we were meeting each other for the first time. We had all become shy. Eva looked gently from my mother to Asa and then to me.

"I would love to see the back garden and the sundial just one more time."

My mother and Asa followed her as she made her way to the kitchen and out the back door.

For a moment or two I hesitated.

I could not bear to say goodbye. I was ashamed of myself for having been so selfish and angry with Eva after Dr. Arendt had left.

I stood at the bottom of the stairs near Eva's handbag. I imagined myself holding the *Augsburg Miscellany*. It was such a vivid image, as if I were standing outside myself, watching from afar as a stranger might.

I began to panic. I could not breathe and felt a terrible pain in my chest.

I could not bear being alone in the house.

"OH, JOSEPH," Eva said, when I came out into the garden.

Everyone was standing around the sundial. For a moment none of us was able to speak. My mother and Asa were crying. My mother blew her nose into her white linen handkerchief.

Finally Asa could not help himself and rushed to Eva, holding her tightly around the waist with his slender arms.

"Oh, Eva, Eva . . . why are you leaving?"

She paused a moment, then said, "I'll miss you most, Asa." Until that moment she had not cried, but now her eyes were moist.

"Then why can't you stay?"

She did not answer his question. She bent over and lifted off the great square of sheer blue silk he wore over his head and eyes. It fluttered between them like a ghost.

She brought her face close to his. "You have brought me such joy, Asa. Did you know that? Now look at me carefully. Look, Asa, so you don't forget."

She smoothed his hair back. His face was damp with tears.

"You won't forget me, Asa?"

He shook his head. "No."

"Never?"

"Never, Eva."

She kissed him on the forehead, keeping her lips there a long time.

She stood up again and turned to embrace me. "You have helped me in many ways, Joseph. You are strong. I will always be grateful."

After that she took my mother in her arms. She whispered in her ear, "I will never forget your kindness, Adele. Forgive me if I have been too selfish."

"Oh, no, no," my mother said. "I never thought that."

Eva stepped back and smiled.

She then embraced each of us again, first Asa, then me, and at last my mother, slowly, gently, this time without words.

We did not follow her back into the house or out again to the car. It would have been unbearable.

A few moments later we heard Dr. Fairclough's station wagon drive away.

CHAPTER 29

FTER EVA WAS GONE, WE ALL sat around the sundial in the garden chairs, my mother and Asa weeping quietly. I was in great pain and still I did not cry. I do not remember how long we sat there. It seemed a very long time. Finally my mother said very softly, "We have to get ready now, boys. It's getting late."

We walked out the front door and down the porch stairs. We passed under the trellis of Gracious Majesties, which still had many blooms left although they were clearly past their days of glory. I sensed they were sad but I was indifferent to their suffering. My own sadness seemed so much greater and more unbearable.

After all, their memories were short and they would not suffer long.

We walked on silently to the synagogue. It was a hot and brilliant morning. Heartbroken, we passed beneath one shady tree canopy after another.

I kept looking back in the direction of our house.

From time to time my mother stopped to catch her breath.

When we arrived at the synagogue the Torah had already been taken from the ark. It was being escorted through the sanctuary by Rabbi Kremlach and several other men.

There was a faint murmur in the congregation. Everyone turned to look as Asa and I entered the men's section, and my mother walked down the aisle of the women's section.

Rabbi Kremlach made an audible sigh of relief. "Oh, Joseph!" I heard him say.

I did not go to my seat but rather hurried to the *bimah*, where the Torah was now being laid down. Its silver ornaments—its turret-shaped finials and filigreed shield—and then its embroidered mantle, gold on blue velvet, were removed.

My mother sat down in the front of the women's section. She was watching me carefully, perched forward on the edge of her seat. She held her *chumash* in her hands. Her eyes were still red.

The large Torah scroll was rolled open before me. Someone said a blessing. I took up the silver pointer and looked down into the great parchment sea.

To my dismay, all the letters and words just lay there in

a jumble. They were all indistinguishable to me. They floated in and out of view, became faded and blurred. I could not remember what the letters represented or why I was there.

My face was burning. I could not read or even move. I stood with the silver pointer in my lifted hand hovering above the Torah.

I did not know what to do.

Then I heard a slow voice from the women's section. It was my mother's voice, her patient voice that had always spoken kindly to my father and to Eva, to Asa and to me.

I heard my mother call out each word by densely syntactic word. Although she must have been speaking quite loudly for me to hear her in the sanctuary, her voice sounded gentle and kind. It was her voice and the voice of her father before her.

There was a hush in the congregation, as if people were straining desperately to hear the news of their future, for the future of the world as well as its past are hidden in the Torah.

"'V'yisu . . . mairamses . . . va'yachanu . . . b'sukkos . . . And they traveled . . . from Ramses . . . and they encamped . . . in Sukkos.'"

Slowly, slowly, my mother fed me the words of the Torah one by one, pausing between each while I repeated them back to the congregation.

"'V'yisu . . . m'sukkos . . . And they traveled . . . from Sukkos . . . and encamped . . . in Eisom . . . which is at the edge of the desert.'"

At first I repeated the words without actually reading

them from the Torah as I was obligated to do. I did not com-
prehend their simple meaning. I was merely imitating sounds
as my mother believed Nebuchadnezzar did. I simply followed my mother's voice, because my eyes were now filled
with tears and I could not see.

And as my mother continued to read to me, her voice
carrying across the sanctuary, the holy letters began to swim
back into view, reasserting themselves on the pale parchment of the open scroll.

The letters and words stood upright in row after row
with their glorious crowns and gracious adornments, as noble kings and gentle queens proudly surveying their domin-
ions. They looked up at me. They spoke to me in their royal
language and sang to me their sovereign music.

Together they told of themselves and of their ancient
story, a story carried on from former times, born over and
over again in our world, preserved in every generation and in
the life of all created things.

And they told of Eva, of her wandering soul with its
storehouse of knowledge and garments of splendor, with its
unbearable longings and moments of sorrow. It was the
story, too, of the life I would certainly lead, the pilgrim life
that all who come into this world are destined to share.

SOON I WAS CALM and clear-headed. I wiped my
tears and read the remainder of the *parsha* on my own. I did
not make any mistakes.

While I was still reading, without looking up from the

parchment, I sensed to my great joy that Eva had come into the synagogue, to the row where my mother was now quietly sitting.

She gently embraced my mother.

I imagined myself saying, You have come back!

When I was done reading, I dared to look up.

Eva was not there.

I told myself, Perhaps she has come and gone.

I realized it was not true. I felt the most terrible pain, a pain that has lessened over time but has never left me completely.

NOW, ALL THESE DECADES LATER, I go from congregation to congregation, reading from my own slender book, *The Illuminated Soul*, no more than the woven images of all the good things I have encountered in my life, preserved as best I might outside the confines of my ephemeral, material brain. After a lifetime of searching, I still do not know where our memories find their home within us, or where they might go after we are dead.

I look up now and see Eva.

How wonderful that she has come back to me.

If only she would stay. If only she would wait until I am finished reading and speaking to the congregation before me.

If only she would stay, I would open my briefcase and take out the *Augsburg Miscellany*.

I would go to her.

Here it is, Eva. I'm sorry.

I thought you would forget me.

I thought I could hold you, though I know now that memory and love—those bright, persistent mirrors—can never capture another's soul.

Would that I had known this then.

Would that all God's people were prophets.

Yet what you told us once is true:

Anything you have ever seen or heard or held in your hand changes you forever.

When we encounter each other, we become part of each other.

I like to imagine that in the end I have helped you. I took upon myself the burden, which you bore for so many years. I have always been unworthy, but for this treasure, which we preserved at an unbearable, unknowable cost.

Perhaps it is what you wished.

Perhaps you knew I would protect the miscellany and its visions.

Would that I had known this then.

Would that all God's people were prophets.

All my life I have never seen anything so beautiful.

Please forgive me. I once judged you harshly. All my life I have borne the sin of ingratitude.

I never thanked you for what you gave us.

For a short while, a long time ago, we were like those celestial beings, arrayed in the higher realms, looking out over the heavens, and we saw so much farther than we had ever imagined.

ACKNOWLEDGMENTS

I wish to thank the many people who in various and often indispensable ways have helped me during the writing of *The Illuminated Soul:* Tobias Picker, Barbara and Merton Bernstein, Kathleen and Glenn Cambor, Pedro and Cory de Armas-Kendall, Marsha Lynn Gordon, Dieter Hall, Deborah Harris, Yuko Ishikura, Eva Jägel-Guedes, Mary Jurisson, Tamar Leiter, Rachel Levy, Henriette Simon Picker, Orlando Rodriguez, Nina Ryan, Lois Rosenthal, Patti Sacher, and Salomão Segal.

I am particularly grateful to my extraordinary editor, Celina Spiegel, for her guiding wisdom and patient encouragement.

A special thanks to the Deputy Prime Minister of Canada, the Honorable Herb Gray, and to his assistant, John Haffner, for their generous help in researching Canadian immigration policy following the Second World War. *The Illuminated Soul* is a work of fiction, and no conclusions should be drawn from it as to actual historical facts and laws.

In the writing of this novel, I have drawn from several remarkable sources: The passage on Evening Faces is adapted from Edward Seidensticker's superb translation of Murasaki Shikibu's *The Tale of Genji* (Knopf, 2000). The Midrash on the city of Jericho is loosely adapted from *The Book of the Cave Treasures* of Ephraem Syrus (306–373 C.E.), cited in *Through the Labyrinth: Designs and Meanings over 5,000 Years* by Hermann Kern (Prestel, 2000). The poem of praise to the qilin was inspired by Shen Du's laudatory hymn commemorating the presentation of a giraffe to the Ming court, cited in *When China Ruled the Seas: The Treasure Fleet of the Dragon Throne, 1405–1433* by Louise Levathes (Oxford University Press, 1996).